Kappy King and the Pie Kaper

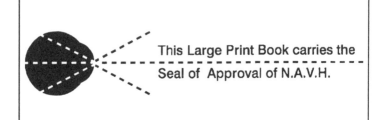

This Large Print Book carries the
Seal of Approval of N.A.V.H.

KAPPY KING AND THE PIE KAPER

AMY LILLARD

THORNDIKE PRESS
A part of Gale, a Cengage Company

Farmington Hills, Mich • San Francisco • New York • Waterville, Maine
Meriden, Conn • Mason, Ohio • Chicago

GALE
A Cengage Company

Copyright © 2019 by Amy Lillard.
An Amish Mystery #3.
Thorndike Press, a part of Gale, a Cengage Company.

ALL RIGHTS RESERVED
This book is a work of fiction. Names, characters, places, and incidents
are either products of the author's imagination or are used fictitiously.
Any resemblance to actual persons, living or dead, events, or locales is
entirely coincidental.
Thorndike Press® Large Print Christian Mystery.
The text of this Large Print edition is unabridged.
Other aspects of the book may vary from the original edition.
Set in 16 pt. Plantin.

LIBRARY OF CONGRESS CIP DATA ON FILE.
CATALOGUING IN PUBLICATION FOR THIS BOOK
IS AVAILABLE FROM THE LIBRARY OF CONGRESS

ISBN-13: 978-1-4328-6226-8 (hardcover)

Published in 2019 by arrangement with Zebra Books, an imprint of
Kensington Publishing Corp.

Printed in Mexico
2 3 4 5 6 7 23 22 21 20 19

To Rob
Thanks for being my Jack.
You are stronger than you know,
braver than you even believe,
and smarter than you think.
And I love you!

CHAPTER 1

"Did you hear?" Edie Peachey shut her car door, then opened it again to shut off the engine. She pushed the door closed and started toward the porch where Kappy waited.

Kathryn King, known to most in her small Amish community in Blue Sky, Pennsylvania, as Kappy, propped her hands onto her hips and eyed her friend. "Hi, Edie. So good to see you, too. Yes, the weather has been nice lately, but September always is, don't you think?"

Edie ignored her sarcasm and plowed ahead. "Alma Miller fell out of her cherry tree and is in a coma."

It could have been the last thing Kappy expected her to say, but something seemed off. Edie was about the best friend Kappy had ever had. The murder of Edie's mother had pulled them together and bonded them in a strong way. The pair had left no stone unturned as they tried to clear Edie's brother of the charges. Yet despite Edie's conservative upbringing — she had been raised Amish, then left to live among the English — she had the tendency to be a bit dramatic in both action and appearance. Like today's outfit of black-and-white-checkered pants and a bright red shirt made out of stretchy material that clung to her in a way that made Kappy a bit uncomfortable. She supposed Edie didn't dress any more risqué than the other English women Kappy encountered. At least her clothes matched today, though the top clashed with Edie's swirly cotton-candy-colored hair.

"Did you put blue in your hair?" She had dyed it pink a couple of months back and it had taken this long for Kappy to get used to it. Now this!

"Just a bit. Did you hear what I said?"

"I did." But still the words seemed impossible. "Where did you hear such a thing?"

Edie hooked one finger back over her shoulder toward the main road. "I was at the Super Saver, and I heard Mary Ann Peachey and Bertha Troyer talking about it."

"You haven't been back a year and already you are falling victim to idle gossip."

Edie cocked her head to one side. "I never

said Mary Raber was involved."

"Like it matters."

Everyone knew that Mary Raber was the biggest gossip in the village of Blue Sky, but that didn't mean there weren't amateurs out there jockeying for her title.

Jockeying. That was her word for the day in her word-a-day calendar. And she thought she would never have the opportunity to use that one. Just goes to show. Kappy loved her calendar. The Amish might only attend school until the eighth grade, but one should never stop learning. At least that's what she thought.

"Coma," Edie said again slowly. "I think you missed that important detail the first go around."

"I heard it." Kappy took a step back to let Edie into the house, then she whistled for Elmer. The pup stopped sniffing at a particularly interesting blade of grass at the edge of the drive. He raised his snout into the air, back leg raised and tail out in the perfect beagle "point." "Come on," she called.

Elmer raced toward her, ears floating on the breeze as he ran. He was getting big, losing his puppy coat and changing colors the way beagles were prone to do. White paws had gained freckles of brown. His ears, once dark silky black, were now a rusty velvet brown. Even the white strip down the center of his face seemed to have shifted. But inside he was all mischievous puppy.

"And you're not concerned for our friend?" Edie continued after Kappy had shut the door behind them.

Elmer raced to the kitchen to get a drink of water, then collapsed in front of the hearth to chew on a rawhide bone. He held it between his front paws as he gnawed on it from the side. Kappy had learned the hard way: It was get him something to chew on or keep buying new shoes.

"I'm considering the source." There was no proof anywhere that any of this were true, but as usual, Edie had fallen into her typical drama-filled response. "And the Millers don't have a cherry tree."

Edie waved a hand around as if erasing Kappy's logic. "Details, details."

But if that information was incorrect, then what else was?

"Besides, I think the preacher's wife and the deacon's wife would know."

Kappy stopped. Neither woman was prone to gossip, but it had been a slow fall. Well, things had slowed down after Sally June Esh was run off the road, but this was another matter altogether. "They don't have a cherry tree."

Edie shrugged. "So she fell out of some other kind of tree. Coma," she repeated, even slower this time.

The last thing Kappy wanted to do was jump to conclusions, but her heart sank despite her resolve. Alma Miller . . . in the hospital? In a coma? "Maybe we should go check it out. When did this happen?"

"Yesterday," Edie said with a nod. "Maybe the day before."

Two days? Where had she been that she was just now hearing about this? Kappy didn't have an answer for that. She had been right where she was now, but she had always been a little on the outside of her community. Sometimes she heard news right after it happened and sometimes she would only find out about it at their every-other-week church services.

"So . . . ?" Edie asked.

Kappy jerked herself out of her thoughts and eyed her friend. She and Edie were a mismatched pair to be certain, but ever since she had returned to Blue Sky, Edie had become more than just a friend. She was Kappy's best friend. Something Kappy hadn't had in a long time. Kappy swallowed hard and nodded. "*Jah.* Let's go to the hospital and see what we can find out."

"I'll drive," Edie said.

Once again Kappy nodded and a worried frown puckered Edie's brow. "You aren't even going to argue about it?"

"Not today." It was a standing disagreement between the two of them. Since Edie had left the church, she drove around in a fancy English car. Well, Kappy supposed it wasn't all that fancy as far as cars went, but it was fancy to her nonetheless.

"Are you sure you're feeling all right?" Edie took a step toward her and pressed the back of one hand to Kappy's forehead, as if to check for fever. "You don't feel warm."

Kappy smacked her hand away. "I'm fine. I would just like to . . ." She would just like to what? Know as soon as possible. There had been too many tragedies in Blue Sky lately and if this one happened not to be true, she wanted to know as soon as humanly possible. "Go," she finally said.

Edie tossed her hair out of her face and nodded. "I have to take Jimmy to work in a bit. I'll get him, then swing back by and we'll go over to the hospital, 'kay?"

"Sure."

Edie shot her one last concerned look and headed out the front door.

Kappy stood where she was for a moment, a silent prayer for Alma running through her mind. How she hoped that Alma had no need, but two days with the same rumor floating around meant one thing: There was some truth in it after all. But how much?

She supposed she would find out soon enough. Or she would find out when they got to the hospital that someone was making things up. As much as she hated a wasted trip, she kind of hoped that would happen. She hated the thought of something bad happening to Alma. She was as sweet as they came. Though if Kappy was being perfectly honest, Alma was a bit prideful over her pies.

She sighed. Once again human nature won out over the church.

Elmer abandoned his chew toy and ran toward the door, stopping short and sniffing the air before plopping his rear down and howling. She didn't think Edie would be back yet, but she never really knew with her friend. And though Kappy was constantly reminding people that she didn't do business from her front porch, inevitably someone came around and knocked.

"Around back," she called. "Down the basement."

"I don't need a prayer *kapp.* I just want to talk to you," the male voice returned. And it wasn't Edie's brother Jimmy Peachey.

"Jack Jones," she said.

"The one and only," he said. At least that's what she thought he said. It was hard to hear with all the noise her dog was making.

"Hush," she told Elmer and stepped over him to the door. Except Elmer picked that time to move and Kappy ended up thumping hard against wall. "Crazy dog," she muttered, then wrenched open the door.

As expected, Jack Jones stood on the porch. Jack was tall and swarthy (last month's word), the image of a pirate, if they still existed like in the old days. His eyes were so dark she could barely see their pupils. The hair on his head was the color of a raven's wing and that on his face was black as well. Not that he had a beard. It just seemed that no matter when she saw him he always had stubble, like his facial hair resented being shaved off and grew back almost immediately. "Everything okay?" he asked.

"*Jah.* Sure." Kappy ran her hands down her front, smoothing out her apron.

"I thought I heard something."

She shook her head. "Just graceful me tripping over this terrible dog." The smile on her face and the affection in her voice took all the sting from her words. "What brings you out this way, Detective?"

14

He hesitated and for the first time since Kappy had met him, Jack looked . . . uncertain. "Is Edie here?" he asked.

She shook her head.

He looked almost relieved. "Can I talk to you about something? Inside?"

She stepped back so Jack could enter. "Of course." But she couldn't stop the small frown of concern that wrinkled her brow. Jack uncertain was one thing but needing to talk to her privately was another matter altogether.

Jack moved past her and into her living room. He shifted from one foot to the other, that cop confidence momentarily put on hold.

"What do you want to talk about?" Kappy asked. All this shifting was making her nervous.

"I suppose you heard about Alma Miller."

She nodded and motioned for him to take a seat on the couch while she settled down in her favorite rocking chair. "Edie said something about it earlier. That she fell out of her cherry tree and was in a coma."

"She had some head trauma and is in a coma, yes," Jack said.

Which was not exactly falling from a possibly nonexistent cherry tree. "So she didn't fall out of a tree? I told Edie the Millers didn't have a cherry tree. Now a crab apple tree . . ."

That was one thing she knew was on their property. Alma Miller was famous in the valley for her crab apple pie recipe. Well, all her pies really. Every year she took first place at the fall festival with her mouth-watering efforts. She claimed fresh ingredients were the secret, but Kappy had a feeling there was more to it than that.

"I can't discuss the particulars of her case with you, but I do need to ask you a question."

"Okay," Kappy stammered. She'd had her doubts about the seriousness or even the validity of Alma's accident, but this just proved it.

Validity. That was another one from her calendar. Kappy loved her word-a-day calendar, but validity was one she never thought she would get to put into practice.

Jack pulled an envelope from inside his jacket and shook something out. After a moment Kappy realized they were photographs.

She shook her head. "I don't want —" She didn't finish that thought. She had no desire to look at the images if they were of what she thought they were. She didn't need to see Alma bent and broken on the ground outside her house. It was simply too much.

Jack ignored her protests and started to lay the pictures out on the coffee table where she could clearly see them. She didn't want to look, but she didn't seem to be able to help herself. But they weren't of poor Alma laying under a cherry-possibly-crab-apple tree. They were of the inside of the house.

Kappy relaxed a bit and let her eyes take in the images before her. The pictures all showed the same thing. It took her a minute to determine exactly what she was looking at. It was the floor of Alma's kitchen. The worn yellow linoleum was covered with flour, as if it had been spilled by a child who then ran through the mess, scattering it about. The pictures may have been of the same subject, but they had been taken from every angle imaginable. In one, she could see the old-fashioned tin cannister that Alma kept her flour in. She brought it to every pie competition every year and Kappy recognized it from that. In another, she could just make out the legs of the kitchen table along with a couple of the chairs. But each seemed to focus on the spread of flour.

"She fell in her house?" Kappy asked. All the rumors had indicated she had been outside. But if this was an accident, then

17

why was the police involved?

"Can you make out these words?"

Kappy squinted at one of the pictures on the top of the pile. "Did someone draw in the flour?" she hesitantly asked. The thought was ridiculous, but she asked regardless.

Jack cleared his throat. "Something like that." He shifted in his seat and Kappy realized that his lack of confidence could be contributed to concern over how much he should say to her.

She turned her gaze from the photographs to Jack. "Why are you telling me all this?"

"There were words, symbols maybe, drawn in the spilled flour."

Kappy gasped. "You think she was attacked and her attacker left a message in the flour?" The thought almost had her jumping to her feet. Somehow she contained her surprise.

"I might have expected this from Edie," Jack grumbled.

"Is that a no?"

"It's a no." Jack pinched the bridge of his nose as if he was starting to get a headache. "We believe that Alma wrote a message in the flour before she lost consciousness."

Kappy nodded. "That makes more sense. *Jah.*" She blamed Edie. She was always running around coming up with crazy ideas about this, that, and the other, but Kappy could forgive her. Edie was merely bored in their quiet village after so many years living among the English.

"Is Alma going to be okay?" she asked.

Jack gave a small shrug. "We don't know. And this may be the only clue we have to finding out who did this."

"So she was attacked." The thought sent shivers all through her. It was hard enough to think of the bishop's poor wife falling from her favorite fruit tree, but taken down in her own house . . .

"I didn't say that."

He didn't have to. If this were nothing more than a simple accident, like tripping over the cat, then Jack Jones would be off talking to someone else about another crime in the village. Instead, he was here . . .

"What are the clues?" Kappy finally asked.

"You know I can't —"

"Discuss the particulars of the case. *Jah,* I know. But was it a B&E?" She wasn't sure where she had picked up the term, but she was self-satisfied that she had found an opportunity to use it in conversation.

He seemed reluctant, then went ahead and answered. "Nothing seems to be missing. There were no signs of forced entry."

"Of course not," Kappy said. "Bishop Sam

never locked his doors."

"Never?"

"He said it was a sign of lack of faith."

Jack's forehead puckered into a small frown. "What does lack of faith have to do with it?"

"It's all part of trusting God and accepting His will."

Jack seemed to think this over for a moment. "I guess." He didn't sound convinced.

"Preacher Sam used to always tell him, 'Do not put thy Lord God to the test.' " A small smile pulled at her lips. The two had been at odds over the matter as long as she could remember.

"Who else knows that they don't lock their doors?"

Kappy raised one shoulder in a half shrug. "Everyone, I guess. I mean, it's never been a secret or anything."

"Well, that doesn't help much."

Kappy glanced back down at the photographs still spread across her coffee table. "Why are you showing these to me?" she finally asked. It was the one question about the entire exchange that had her confused.

"We're having trouble figuring out what the words mean. I thought perhaps they could be Pennsylvania Dutch."

She picked up one of the images and

studied it. She hadn't noticed it before, but there, in the mounds of powdery white flour, she could just make out a word. She carefully placed it back and picked up the next photograph.

"Is it?"

"Is it what?" Kappy asked. She was so intent on studying the picture that she lost the thread of the conversation.

"Dutch." A small note of irritation colored his voice.

"You know Edie speaks Dutch as well."

He nodded. "I know."

But he didn't want to ask her. That much was obvious.

Kappy waited, hoping that if she stalled long enough Jack would crack and tell her exactly why he didn't want to tell Edie.

"Well?" he asked.

"Why didn't you take these to Edie to interpret?" she finally asked outright.

"Really?"

As far as answers went, it wasn't exactly what she had hoped.

They sat in silence for a full moment before Jack finally spoke.

"Can you read it or not? I mean, we thought it was Pennsylvania Dutch, but it could be another language."

"It is," Kappy said. "It's English."

21

Jack blinked at her as if the movement of his lids would bring all the wayward pieces back into focus. "What?"

"It's English." She tapped the photograph with her index finger. "Alma has always had the worst penmanship." She stopped, shook her head. "Do you still call it penmanship if she wrote it with her finger? She did write it with her finger, right?"

Jack didn't answer, just tugged the photo from her grasp and studied it. "This is English?" he asked. She was sure to clarify one last time.

"Without a doubt."

"Is that a nine?" he asked.

Kappy peered to where he pointed to a spot on one of the pictures. "Looks like it to me."

"And this says . . ." He hesitated as he tried to make out the letters. "Babies?"

"That's what I see."

Jack frowned. "*Nine babies?* What does that mean?"

Kappy opened her mouth to respond, but he waved her words away before she could even say them. "Rhetorical."

And because of her word-a-day calendar she knew exactly what that meant.

"And I think the other words are *ME* and *blue.*"

He shook his head and mumbled some-thing that sounded a lot like "that doesn't make any sense at all."

And it didn't. "What do you suppose it means?" Kappy asked.

Jack gathered up the pictures and rose to his feet. "Thanks for your help, Kappy."

"Uh," she sputtered and pushed to her feet as well. Like a puppy, she followed behind Jack to the door. Ironically, Elmer trotted behind her, tail wagging. "You're welcome."

Jack flashed her that smile of his, then loped down the porch steps.

"Is Alma going to be all right?"

"Hard to say." Jack had reached his car. He opened the door and slid behind the wheel. Before she could ask even one more question, he backed out of her drive and with a small wave, he disappeared down the road.

Kappy was sitting on her porch, purse in hand when Edie arrived ten minutes later.

"Are you ready to go?" Edie called from the driver's seat.

"Hi, Kappy!" Jimmy called from the back.

"*Jah,*" she said. "Hi, Jimmy." Then she made her way to the car.

She'd had ten long minutes to think about

Jack and Alma and all his questions, even though he answered none of hers. Concern for Alma was number one in her thoughts, but if Jack was involved . . .

That couldn't be right. Jack worked more in homicides. This wasn't one. This was an accident. Except Alma hadn't fallen out of a tree of any type. She had written her message in the house. A message not about who had possibly attacked her but babies and colors. It was beyond strange.

"You're awfully quiet," Edie said.

"Hmmm?" Kappy turned her attention to her friend, only then realizing that they were halfway to Mose Peachey's bait shop, where Jimmy worked part-time.

Edie had encouraged him to take the job to help him socialize more. He had plenty of work to do on their farm. Besides the garden and housework, they had the beagles to take care of along with the plethora of animals that Jimmy had taken in. Ducks, gerbils, rabbits, and goats. Though he had yet to convince his sister that he needed to raise miniature pigs. According to Edie, his assortment was big enough.

Plethora. She smiled a little and gave herself a mental pat on the back for remembering it. *Plethora* was one of her calendar words from last week.

"Why?" Edie asked.

Kappy thought for a moment about playing dumb but shrugged instead. "Just thinking." Plus, Jimmy had chattered away almost nonstop since they had started on down the road. With him rambling on about this and that, she didn't feel the need to add anything else. Instead she had begun to wonder about all the things Jack Jones had told her that afternoon. Or maybe it was what he hadn't said.

Alma had been attacked in her own home. With what? She didn't know, but now the bishop's wife was in the hospital, condition unknown.

"What is it?" Edie asked.

"Huh?" Kappy swung her attention back to Edie.

"Something's wrong. What is it?"

Kappy scoffed and waved a hand as if flicking away her suspicions. "Nothing's wrong. Why would anything be wrong?"

"You tell me. We've been in this car for fifteen minutes and you haven't criticized my driving once, nor have you clutched the dash like your life depended on it. So spill it."

"It's nothing really. Just a . . . new covering pattern I'm working on in my head."

"Uh-huh," Edie said slowly, then turned

her attention back to the road. Kappy didn't even have to ask her to do so. Because Edie's driving was improving? Hardly. Because Kappy had entirely too much running around in her head. And anything she might want to tell Edie . . . well, she didn't want to discuss such matters in front of Jimmy. He reminded them daily that he was grown up and not a kid anymore, but there was no sense scaring him if she didn't have to. And surely finding out that one of the sweetest ladies in their district had been attacked in her own home would frighten the pants off anyone.

"We can talk about it later," Kappy finally said. She cut her eyes toward the back seat, but she wasn't sure Edie had seen the movement.

No matter. Edie turned the car into the packed gravel parking area of the bait shop.

"I get off at three," Jimmy reminded her as he let himself out of the car. "Don't be late."

"I won't," Edie promised.

A few months before, Edie had been late to pick up Jimmy from work and he'd been really distressed, threatening to press the call button on his emergency alert necklace the next time Edie was late. Of course it didn't help that it was also the day Sally

26

June Esh had been run off the road while she was delivering church pickles for her family's business. Jimmy hadn't let Edie forget it despite all the times she had taken him and picked him up on time since then.

"Bye, Kappy."

She waved in return and watched as Jimmy let himself into the small shed that served as a store.

Once he was out of sight, Edie turned toward her. "Okay. He's gone. Spill it."

Kappy thought about it a moment, just trying to figure out the best place to start.

She must have taken too long for Edie goosed her in the side.

"Argh!" Kappy jumped and yelped, hugging the door to get out of her reach. "Okay, okay. Give me a second."

Edie retreated and Kappy used the small reprieve to smooth her prayer *kapp* back into its proper place. "Jack Jones came by today."

"Jack?" Edie's eyes turned smoky with just the mention of his name. "When? After I left?"

Kappy nodded, and left out that he had made sure Edie was nowhere around before coming in.

"What did he say?"

She shrugged, wondering perhaps if she

27

was making too big a deal out of this. "He showed me some pictures and wanted to know if I knew what the words meant."

Edie shook her head. "You lost me."

"He had pictures of the crime scene where Alma was attacked. Someone had written in the flour. They assume it was Alma, and they wanted to know if it was Dutch."

Edie simply stared at her for a moment. "Alma was attacked?"

Kappy nodded. "Apparently someone broke into her house and conked her on the head."

CHAPTER 2

"What?" Edie's eyes widened. "Why am I just now hearing about this?"

"I don't know. I just heard about it myself."

Edie frowned at her. "You heard about it almost an hour ago!"

"Only because Jack needed my help."

Edie snorted.

"Someone wrote some words in the flour. See, I suppose Alma was baking when whoever hurt her came in. She had her flour tin in her hands or she knocked it off the counter when she fell. I don't really know. But there was flour spilled all over the floor."

"And someone wrote in it."

"Jah."

"Who?"

"Alma? The attacker? How am I supposed to know?"

She seemed to think about that a moment. "And Jack couldn't read whatever it was on his own?"

"He thought it might be Dutch."

Edie fell unusually quiet. "I can read Dutch."

Thankfully, Kappy didn't have to answer. Jimmy came to the door of the bait shop and waved them away. It seemed like having his sister and her best friend hang out in the parking lot in front of where he worked was cramping his independent lifestyle.

Edie waved at him as if to say nothing was amiss, then put the car into gear.

"Are we still going to see Alma?" Kappy asked as Edie stopped at the edge of the lot. She didn't have on her blinker, and Kappy had no idea which way she might turn. The original plan might have been to check on the bishop's wife at the hospital, but with everything that Edie just discovered . . .

"Of course." She set the car in motion and headed for the hospital.

They were almost to the hospital before Edie spoke. "So Alma didn't fall out of the cherry tree."

"I told you," Kappy said. "The Millers don't have a cherry tree."

"Whatever." Edie blew her bangs out of her face, a sure sign she was frustrated and doing her best to pretend that everything was fine. "Whatever kind of tree it was, she didn't fall out of it."

It took a full fifteen seconds for Kappy to decipher that sentence. She nodded. "It sounds to me like she was in her house, minding her own business, and bam. Someone hit her with something."

"Did Jack say why? I mean, it's not like she has a television or a computer. She doesn't even have one of those ridiculous five-hundred-dollar mixer machines."

"There wasn't anything else taken." And when she thought about it like that, it made her wonder: Why would someone break into the Millers' house, beat on Alma, then leave? If that were truly the case, it would be like someone did it for the sole purpose of harming the sweet lady.

"People do a lot of crazy things," Edie said as if she could read her mind.

"You don't think . . ." Kappy trailed off, unable to finish the question.

"That someone only wanted to hurt her?" Edie shrugged. "It's weird, though, huh?" She pulled into the hospital parking lot and slipped her car into the closest spot she could find.

"I mean, this is Alma Miller we're talking about."

Edie shut off the car and got out, leaving Kappy to follow. "So it was just a robbery gone bad." She said the words as if that was all there was to it. But doubts still plagued Kappy. Why?

"So what did it say?" Edie asked as they entered the large glass doors.

"What?"

"The message in the flour. Didn't you say Alma left a message?"

"I didn't know for certain . . ." Kappy hedged.

"So someone breaks into their house. He or she hits Alma over the head with something, then stops to write a message? *And* leaves the vic breathing on the floor?"

"The vic?" Kappy asked as they stepped into the elevator.

"You know, victim." Edie shrugged. "What room?"

Kappy dug into her purse for the note she had written about Alma's room number and what floor she was on, then rattled it off to Edie.

The doors closed behind them.

"So?" Edie asked again.

It took Kappy a moment to regain the thread of the question. "It was weird. Something about nine blue babies."

"That doesn't make any sense at all."

"I know," Kappy said. "I may be remembering wrong. Either way, Jack is a professional. I'm sure he'll figure out what it means soon."

"Yeah," Edie said. "Soon." She shook her head. "Nine blue babies?"

"Your guess is as good as mine on that one."

Alma had been put into a medical coma in order to allow her brain and body time to heal. Kappy and Edie weren't allowed into visit. That, plus the way the doctors delivered the news, seemed to indicate that this was an unlikely scenario.

"Poor Alma," Edie whispered as they sat in the waiting room with the others. There were several people she didn't know, plus Preacher Sam and a few prominent members of their church. And Alma's sister, Rose Menno. Their sister Nancy lived in Lancaster and would probably come in soon. For the first time in a great while, Kappy thought about Alma's other sister, Amelia. But Amelia had left Blue Sky long ago. Kappy wondered if anyone had told her about Alma. Or if she was even still alive.

Kappy let her gaze wander around the room once more. She supposed not everyone was there waiting for news about Alma

Miller. Not that there was any news coming. But the pair had decided to stay for a minute rather than zipping in and back out again without stopping for just a few minutes.

Now they waited for the time when they could leave without raising any consternation from the other church members. Edie couldn't have cared less, but Kappy was thankful that she stuck around for her.

Edie leaned a bit closer and whispered out of the corner of her mouth. "Can we go now?"

Kappy lifted her chin a tad and looked from side to side. She had bowed her head as if in prayer. She had prayed, but this time was more about solemn respect than an actual plea to the Lord. "Let someone else get here and we'll go."

Edie made an unladylike noise that drew the attention of two of their fellow waiters. She smiled and gave them an apologetic wave. "That could be hours," she protested.

It was true. They didn't have to pick Jimmy up for a while, but Kappy wanted to be out of the sad hospital long before Jimmy got off from work. "Just let something happen," she finally said. "We'll slip out during the commotion."

"I'll give you commotion." Before Kappy

could protest, Edie stood, stretched big, and yawned even bigger. "Whew. I think I need a breath of fresh air. What about you, Kappy?"

What choice did she have but to answer? By the end of her first sentence, all eyes were on Edie. Kappy rose to her feet. "I suppose that would be good."

She shook hands with Preacher Sam but didn't approach the bishop. He was standing alone looking out the window. He had been standing there for quite some time, but Kappy didn't know if he was contemplative or praying. Either way, she felt it best to allow him some measure of privacy.

And in no time at all, she and Edie were back out in the early fall sunshine.

"It just doesn't make any sense," Edie said as they drove home.

"Does anything like this ever make sense?" Kappy asked.

"Well, no, but I mean this *really* doesn't make sense."

Kappy swung her full attention to her friend. "You're going to have to explain that one."

"I'm not talking about the sad fact that a sweet woman was attacked in her home. Unfortunately, things like that happen every day."

"That's comforting," Kappy snorted.

"I'm talking about the why."

Kappy frowned. "Still not seeing the difference here."

"What did the person who attacked her stand to gain?"

"Is there always a gain?"

Edie shot her a look, then quickly turned her attention back to the road ahead. Kappy breathed a small sigh of relief. "Always."

Kappy thought it over for a minute. She considered herself pretty smart. She read a lot and had a lot more time than most to learn even though she had finished school long ago, but she had to assume that Edie simply had more experience in such matters. After all, she had spent the past ten years among the English. She had learned things, saw things, and heard things that Kappy couldn't imagine. If Edie believed there was always a gain, then Kappy had to accept that it was true. On some level it had to be.

"So what's the gain?" Kappy finally asked.

Edie shrugged one shoulder, her hands loose on the steering wheel. "I have no idea."

"Seriously? Then why did you ask?"

Her friend shot her a ready grin. "I was hoping you could tell me."

"Could we be looking for a why so it's easier for us to accept?"

"I have to admit that the thought of a random crime for no reason, or a criminal out there who doesn't know the difference between the Amish and the English and the treasures they hold dear scares me half to death. But there still should be a reason."

And since Alma was Amish and a conservative yellow-topper at that, there were no televisions, computers, or jewelry. The most valuable thing she owned was most likely her china cabinet and the grandfather clock that was a traditional wedding gift from groom to bride. And perhaps her china itself. All those items would be hard to take out of a home, but not impossible. "What about her china hutch and her grandfather clock?" she finally asked.

"As far as I know, both are still in the house."

So if there was a why, then what was it?

"It just doesn't make sense," Kappy said.

Edie pounded the heel of one hand against her steering wheel. "That's what I've been saying."

Kappy stared out the window, watching the landscape zoom by in a blur of green-slowly-turning-to-brown. Soon fall would have them firmly in hand. The festival would start, and everyone would prepare to enjoy the celebrations. And Alma could possibly still be in the hospital.

Unless they figured out what item of value the person was after. And did they get it? Once again Kappy shook her head.

"What?"

"We're doing it again. *You're* doing it again."

"Doing what again?"

"We don't know for certain that a crime has been committed," Kappy reminded her.

"If there's no crime, then why is Jack involved?"

Kappy folded the morning paper back to rights and sighed as a knock sounded on the front door. Elmer immediately started barking as he trotted over, his tail wagging in proof of how vicious he really was. It was too early for a customer to have violated her "go around back" policy and that could only mean one of three people — Edie, Jimmy, or Jack Jones. Her guess was Jimmy.

She nudged the pup out of her way with one foot and opened the door to find the young man standing there. "And bingo."

Jimmy frowned. "What?"

"Nothing." She smiled at him and stood to one side so he could enter. "What brings you out today?"

Jimmy looked back over one shoulder in the direction where his house lay, but he didn't come inside. "Edie sent me over. She wants to talk to you and says you need to get a phone."

Of course she did. "I'm not getting a phone." Like she could even have one. "Why didn't Edie come down?"

"I wanted to walk anyway." Jimmy shrugged. "Are you coming?"

Did she have a choice? "Let me get Elmer's leash."

Kappy retrieved the leash and the puppy, then locked the door and headed up the road with Jimmy. The morning held the hint of a chill and the smell of hay seemed to surround them. Fall was definitely in the air.

"The festival will be here soon," Jimmy said. Kappy had been thinking the very same thing.

Every year, Blue Sky held a fall festival complete with a pumpkin growing contest, a baking competition, and blue ribbons for the best animals entered. Like everyone else in the valley, she looked forward to the festival every year. She had never entered any of the competitions, but she enjoyed walking through the booths vendors set up to sell everything from pickles to kitchen gadgets. It was also great fun to check out all the quilts made especially for the quilt competition and the art work and photographs entered by the Englishers. It was a time for English and Amish to come together and celebrate another harvest before the holiday and wedding seasons rolled around.

"I was thinking about entering Judith Junior in the competition this year." Judith was his prize rabbit with big floppy ears and the softest fur Kappy had ever felt. She was black and white like a panda with a twitchy nose. Judith Junior was one of her last litter and had become almost as much of a pet to Jimmy as Judith herself. Normally he sold the baby bunnies, but so far, he hadn't been able to part with Judith Junior.

"Is there a rabbit category?" Kappy asked.

He shook his head. "There's a small animal under fifteen pounds category, though."

"What does Edie say?"

Jimmy made a face. "I haven't asked her yet."

"You better," Kappy chided. "Doesn't registration end soon?"

"*Jah.*" But she could tell he was dragging his feet over the whole matter.

"What's wrong?"

"Nothing," he mumbled.

They turned left and headed up the small incline that led to the house. Earlier that year, protestors lined the lane under the false suspicion that the Peacheys' beagle-breeding business was little more than a puppy mill. Nothing could be further from the truth. But it had taken the protestors a long time to be convinced.

"Something's wrong," Kappy said.

"I haven't asked Edie if I can."

Ask? Why should he have to ask? Maybe to get the entry fee, but that was a minimal fee for something Jimmy had his heart set on.

"Then you better get to it," Kappy said.

"Absolutely not," Edie said.

"But why?" Kappy and Jimmy spoke at the same time. They were all seated around the kitchen table eating bagels with cream cheese, something Edie liked to call "second breakfast." She would laugh to herself after she said it. Kappy had yet to understand the humor.

"I don't think it's a good idea." The tone of her voice was one Kappy recognized. That I'm-not-backing-down-so-you-might-as-well-give-up-now quality that Kappy knew all too well.

Jimmy on the other hand, was not ready to let go of his dream. "But Edie . . ." He continued to negotiate with his sister while Kappy tried to disappear without moving. She hadn't thought Edie would react like this.

The pair stood, started talking over each other, Jimmy giving solid and valid reasons why he should be allowed to enter the competition and Edie flat-out refusing.

"No, and that's final." Edie wasn't exactly yelling, but she raised her voice above Jimmy's.

He let out a frustrated growl and slammed out the back door.

Edie raised a hand to her temple and massaged a spot there.

"I'm sorry," Kappy said. "If I had known . . ."

"But you didn't." Edie's tone turned sharp. "Now I'm the one who should apologize."

Kappy waved away her request. "Just tell me one thing. Why not?"

Edie eased back down into her chair and poked her bagel with the end of the cream cheese knife. "What if he loses?"

Kappy sat back in her seat. "If he loses, then he loses."

"But he'll be disappointed and everything. How's he going to handle that?"

"He spent two weeks in jail. I think he can handle not winning a blue ribbon at the fall festival."

Edie pushed away her plate and laid her head on her outstretched arms. "I'm a terrible sister."

Kappy could barely hear the words, muffled as they were. "You're not a terrible sister. Just an overprotective one."

Edie raised her head. "I'm not overprotective."

"*Jah,* you are."

She sat up straight. "I let him have goats."

"After he begged and begged for them."

"And he has a part-time job."

"That you take him to every day."

"What am I supposed to do? Let him drive?" Edie stopped as if shocked by her own words. "Oh, no, no, no, no, no, no, no." She pushed to her feet once again and went to stare out the window. Kappy had stood there enough times to know that she could see all the yard, including the puppy pens and the rabbit hutches, which was most likely where Jimmy had gone after storming out. "No," Edie said again.

Kappy shrugged. "Or you could let him enter his bunny in the fall festival small animal under fifteen pounds competition."

Edie turned around slowly and eyed her with an admiring anger just simmering below the surface. "Anyone ever tell you that you don't play fair?"

"Never," Kappy returned with a smile.

"Here are the rules for the competition." Edie held the papers over her head sometime later. After she had talked with Kappy, she had gone outside to tell Jimmy the good news. Kappy heard his whoop of joy all the way inside.

"Okay." Jimmy squirmed in his chair, his excitement barely contained.

Edie handed the printed pages to him. "If you do this, you'll be responsible for following all these rules."

Kappy was the only one who knew what that allowance had cost her. She smiled at her friend.

"There's sure lots of them," Jimmy said.

"Where did you get them?" Kappy asked.

"I printed them off *Mamm*'s computer in the barn."

Ruth Peachey had been nothing if not a savvy business woman, gaining permission to run her breeding business much in the way an Englisher would. She had a phone line, computer, printer, and anything else she might have needed in the barn. It went a long way in helping Edie pick up the reins after her death.

"This can't be right." Jimmy looked up from his reading, shaking his head.

A moment of hopelessness flashed across Edie's face, then she visibly stiffened her backbone and cleared her throat. "Like them or not, if you want to enter the competition, that's what you have to do."

A frown of confusion puckered his brow. "But it says here that all the entries must be fruit. How can a rabbit be fruit? Do they mean I have to rename him?"

"Let me see that." Edie took the papers from him, scanning them quickly, then going back and reading them over, slower the second time. "It does." She looked at Kappy, her expression incredulous. It was a word meaning *disbelieving.* She had learned it from last year's calendar.

"It does?" Kappy's mouth dropped open. Then she shook her head. "That can't be right."

"It is. Look here." Edie handed the papers to Kappy to read.

She scanned the rules, noting the clause about fruit. "Pies," she said, tapping the paper with her index finger. "This is about pies."

45

Jimmy shook his head. "I don't want to bake my rabbit into a pie."

Kappy wasn't sure if he was joking or serious so she decided to leave that one alone.

"Not possible, bud, seeing as how it has to be made from fruit." She accepted the papers back from Kappy and read them again.

"See?" Kappy said. "It clearly says pies."

Edie shook her head. "I thought that was an abbreviation for something else."

"Uh-huh. Or maybe you should wear your glasses more." Or at all.

Edie made a face and tossed her cotton candy hair. "They don't suit me."

"Neither does squinting everywhere you go, but it hasn't stopped you from doing that." Jimmy laughed heartily at his own joke.

"She doesn't like how they look with her hair," Kappy said to Jimmy.

"Or how she looks in them when she's with Jack Jones."

"Okay, that's quite enough entertainment at my expense." She snatched the papers away from Kappy, squinted at them, then pulled the ones that didn't apply from the stack. "I guess I printed the rules for this year's pie competition, too. Here." She handed half the stack back to Jimmy for him

46

to read. Hopefully it was the half that contained the information about the small animal competition.

"Let me see that." Kappy reached out a hand for the other set of rules. "Did that really just say that they had to make a fruit pie?"

Instead of handing them back, Edie read them over. "It goes further than that. Listen to this. In accordance to the new rules passed for this year's competition, all pies must have fruit filling. The exact fruit shall be determined at the time registration opens."

"Does that mean . . . ?" Kappy asked.

Edie nodded. "I think it means that everyone will be baking the same kind of pie this year."

Each year the pie competition had been held and contestants were able to make their specialty pies. Not that it mattered all that much. Alma Miller won every year with her famous boysenberry pie. There were many in the area that thought her championing of the contest was unfair. At the top of that list was Frannie Lehman.

Frannie had not had it easy. She had been five months pregnant with her sixth child when her husband was killed in a freak silo accident ten years ago. Not knowing how she was going to take care of her family and unwilling to split up her children among family members, Frannie turned to the only profitable skill she had: baking. She opened Frannie's Bakery in her basement and now served up bread, cookies, cakes, brownies, and other tasty treats to the people of Blue Sky and the surrounding villages.

But no matter how much Frannie baked, how yummy her cronuts were, or how much everyone loved her sugar cookies, she could not topple Alma Miller as the pie queen.

She never said as much, but Kappy could tell that it bothered her.

"What about coconut cream pie?" Edie asked.

"What about it?" Kappy returned.

"Is it a fruit?"

Kappy shook her head. "How do I know?"

"And key lime."

"Lime is a fruit."

"So are tomatoes, but I don't think tomato pie will be included."

"Pumpkin." Jimmy looked up from the papers he was reading and wrinkled his nose.

Edie turned back to Kappy. "Yeah, pumpkin. That's a vegetable."

"Pumpkins are gourds."

"Yuck," Jimmy exclaimed with a laugh.

"Gourd pie."

Kappy sighed. "Why are we having this conversation?"

"What pie do you suppose they'll make?" Edie mused.

"I couldn't begin to guess," Kappy returned.

"When will they decide?" Jimmy asked.

His sister turned and gave him a curious look. "You seem very interested in pies."

"Don't they let the people try the pies if there's some left after the judging?"

They did, but a person had to be at the festival at the time of judging and fairly close to the action if they wanted to get so much as a taste.

"I wonder if Alma knows about this new rule."

"I'm sure she does," Edie said.

Which made Kappy wonder how she took the news.

"I wonder why they changed the rules this year. I mean, it seems sort of sudden, don't you think?"

"I wouldn't know," Kappy said.

Edie tapped one finger against her chin in a thoughtful gesture. "What if Frannie petitioned the festival counsel in order to change the rules? She's been trying to beat Alma all these years."

"That's a little out there, don't you think?"

"That would put her at the top of our list of suspects."

Kappy took a calming breath and let it out slowly. "We don't have a list of suspects."

"Of course we do. We can't let someone come in and attack the bishop's wife and not do a thing about it."

"This is the same bishop who shuns you."

Edie sniffed. "That has nothing to do with it."

"It has everything to do with it," Kappy said. "You just like to nose around in other people's business.

"I do not."

"You know what you need?"

"I have a feeling you're going to tell me."

"You need a job."

"I have a job. Beagle breeding, remember?"

"Jimmy takes care of the dogs and the paperwork takes you less than half an hour a day."

"I am not getting a job."

"Fine," Kappy said, crossing her arms in front of her. "I'm not helping you dig around in other people's business."

CHAPTER 3

Nine babies. ME blue.

Kappy stared at the words she had written on the paper, but nothing. No idea came to her as to what it might mean. She didn't know why she was even trying to figure it out. Jack Jones had asked her to translate Alma's writing in the flour and she had done that. Not that it had needed much conversion. Okay, any. But she had helped as requested. That was all she needed to do.

So why was she staring at the words trying to delve into the mystery of who attacked the bishop's wife?

She thumped the end of her pencil against the paper. Nine babies. It had been the number nine, but who had nine babies? Not many. So could Alma have meant *nein,* German for no? She jotted it down on the paper and studied it from this angle, then another. She supposed it was possible seeing as how most Amish knew German on some level.

Even their own language was a derivative of German, but no one said *nein* these days. Simply no.

But Alma had been conked on the head with some object, Kappy wasn't sure what, and could have been a little disoriented. No babies? She wrote that under *nein*. What would no babies have to do with anything? Maybe the attacker had no children. A possibility, but it seemed farfetched. If Alma had the presence of mind to remember the attacker didn't have any children, then why didn't she just write their name in the flour? It surely would have made this part a lot easier.

Kappy blew out a breath and cocked her head to one side. It sounded like a car had pulled up into her driveway. Between Elmer's warning barks, she could tell the engine was turned off, then a knock sounded at the door.

Only one person drove a car to her house.

She rose and opened the door for her friend. "Hey, Edie. What brings you out today?"

Edie raised her nose a bit in the air and stepped into the house. "I had to take Jimmy to work."

"Right." It was Friday, after all. But Kappy usually went with Edie when she took him.

It was fun to get out of the house even if Edie's driving left something to be desired. Okay, a lot to be desired. And Edie not swinging by to pick up Kappy was testament to just how upset she still was about yesterday's conversation.

Edie flounced to the table and plopped down in one of the chairs. "Do you have a paper?" she asked.

"A newspaper?"

"Of course a newspaper. You get the paper, right?"

"*Jah.*" She got the local paper as well as *Die Botschaft* and *The Budget,* the two most popular newspapers for Plain people.

"Can I read it?" Edie waited, but her demeanor was anything but patient.

"Sure. *Jah.*" Kappy turned toward the living room and the coffee table where she had left this morning's edition of the local news. When was Edie going to be over her anger? It wasn't like Kappy meant to offend her, but she knew her friend well enough to know that Edie was bored. She needed a challenge, something more in her life besides being shunned and raising puppies. Maybe she needed a man . . .

"What are you looking for?" Kappy asked as she handed the paper over to Edie.

"I thought I might look for a job so I don't

53

have to butt into everyone's business." She didn't make eye contact as she snapped open the paper. The effect was somewhat ruined since she held it upside down.

"Okay." Kappy raised her hands in the air. "I apologize. I didn't mean it the way it sounded, okay?"

Edie folded down one corner and eyed her skeptically. "Then how did you mean it?"

Kappy eased into the chair opposite Edie. "It's just that . . ." It was just that Edie kept threatening to leave Blue Sky and head back to the English world. Not that she wasn't living a mostly English lifestyle in the middle of the third oldest Anabaptist settlement still in existence. Every time Edie got a little antsy, Kappy worried that her friend had simply grown tired of the limited electricity she had thanks to the secret solar panels she had installed. That she had grown tired of being shunned by the very neighbors she had known all her life. But most of all, Kappy worried what would become of Jimmy. Sure, he had different needs than most, but his mother had been very protective of him. Not that the community itself didn't accept him. Kappy knew firsthand that they did. No, Ruth Peachey had considered Jimmy a special gift from

54

God and she had cherished him. Maybe even a little too much. And Edie seemed determined to continue in her mother's footsteps. As least as far as Jimmy was concerned. And that's what really bothered Kappy. If Edie decided to go back to the city, what would become of him? Edie had promised that she would see to Jimmy no matter what, but Kappy worried all the same.

"I really think you should teach Jimmy how to drive."

A bark of laughter burst from Edie. "I can't teach him how to drive my car."

Kappy shook her head. "No. The buggy. I mean, he needs to be allowed, too. You know, he can drive a buggy." After all, he'd driven over from his house earlier in the year to paint Kappy's door blue. He wanted to make sure that all the bachelors in Blue Sky knew that she was available. He knew as well as everyone else that painting the front door blue meant a woman of marriageable age lived in the house was nothing more than a myth. But bless his heart, he wanted to make certain she had every advantage after she and Hiram called off their wedding.

Edie shook her head and buried her nose back in the paper. She blew out a frustrated breath, turned it right side up, and snapped it open once more.

"Quit." Kappy chopped one hand down the center of the paper. "You and I both know you aren't getting a job."

Edie shot her a *finally, the woman makes sense* look and refolded the paper. Somehow it didn't look quite the same as it had when Kappy handed it to her. "Then why did you say that?"

"Because I want you to stay."

Edie opened her mouth to respond, closed it, then opened it once again. "I told you —"

"I know, I know," Kappy interrupted. "But I . . ." She shook her head. "Never mind." She had been about to plead her case for all the reasons Edie should not leave Blue Sky, shouldn't even think about it, but she decided against it. When Edie made up her mind about something that was that. All Kappy could do was stand back and see how it turned out. And pray that the Lord saw fit to keep her friend right where she was.

"What's that?"

"Huh? What?" Kappy followed the angle of Edie's pointed finger. "Uh, that's a list I made. I mean a note."

"A note about what?"

Kappy reached out to cover the paper where she had been trying to decipher the words Alma had left in the flour, but she was too late. Edie slapped one hand on the notebook and pulled it to her side of the table.

"What is this?"

She really didn't want to answer that. For many reasons. But she knew she would have to. "It's what Alma wrote in the flour after she was attacked."

Edie cocked her head. "This doesn't make sense."

"I told you."

"Why would she write gibberish?" Edie asked.

"I wouldn't call it gibberish," Kappy protested.

"Nine babies. ME blue? Sounds like gibberish to me."

"This was after she was hit on the head. They don't even know if she was coherent enough to actually give them a clue as to who hit her."

"Why wouldn't she just write the name of the person?"

Kappy shrugged. "Maybe the person was still there."

"Or maybe she didn't think anyone would know who it was by their name alone."

Kappy shot her a look. "Seriously? Everybody knows everybody in Blue Sky."

"My point exactly. Gibberish."

"It has to mean something," Kappy countered.

"This means absolutely nothing."

"But —"

A knowing smile spread across Edie's face and Kappy's stomach fell. She knew that look all too well.

"What?" She feigned innocence.

"Nothing, just seems to me like someone is butting into other people's business. Wouldn't you say?"

"No." Kappy recaptured her notebook and placed it on the table in front of her. "Maybe."

Edie laughed. "Maybe. Sure."

"It's just . . ."

"Just what?" Edie asked.

"Why would Alma go to all the trouble of writing a message in the flour at the crime scene if no one is going to know what it means?"

Edie sat back in her chair and tapped one finger against her cheek. "Maybe it's code."

Kappy shook her head. "No one would be able to read code."

"Alma can."

"Alma's in a coma."

"Good point."

"So why?" Kappy asked again.

Edie seemed to mull it over a little more. "Maybe when she was hit, it rattled her brain, and this was all she could think of."

Kappy stopped. Thought about it for a moment. "And these words somehow identify her attacker?"

"It's possible."

And it was. These days around Blue Sky anything was possible.

"What's the ME for?" Edie asked.

"Not sure. It could be me as in I or it could be initials. M. E."

"Like Miriam Ebersol?"

"I suppose. Except that Miriam Ebersol died three years ago."

"Mary Esh?" Edie asked.

Kappy shot her a look and didn't answer.

"I wish I had seen the pictures. Maybe you just thought it said these things."

"Oh, it said them all right." Though it would be easier for them all if the words had been more legible. And made sense. With the tip of one finger, Kappy traced the words she had written on the paper. "Jack's a professional. He'll figure it out."

"We've only got an hour," Edie reminded her. "Then we have to pick up Jimmy."

"You've already said that," Kappy replied from her place in the passenger seat. "Are you sure you don't want to wait until later? I mean, we went to the hospital yesterday to see Alma. No one will expect us to come again today."

"What if they decide to take her off the medications tonight and she goes home tomorrow? Then we'll have missed our chance."

Kappy shifted in her seat. "I'm not sure there is a chance. I'm not even sure why we're going back to the hospital."

Edie shrugged one shoulder, her bright green shirt stretching with the movement. At least it stayed in place. Edie had a tendency to wear shirts with big necks, which caused them to fall off her shoulders. Kappy thought they were designed to fit that way, but to her it was still odd for them to be so . . . lopsided. "We're going back to the hospital to see if anyone says anything suspicious."

"Like who? Bishop Sam?"

"Joke all you want," Edie said primly. "But eighty-five percent of people who are killed are murdered by someone they know."

"Really?" Kappy had no idea.

"Yes. Well, maybe. I mean, it might not be quite eighty-five, but it's up there."

"So you made that up?"

"A little."

They rode in silence for almost a mile.

"Alma wasn't murdered," Kappy said.

"Attacked, then." Edie gave another of her one-shoulder shrugs.

Kappy thought about it a moment. "You think she knew who attacked her?"

"Probably," Edie replied. "Did Jones say if there were signs of forced entry?"

"Why would he?"

"Was anything taken from the house?"

"How would I know?"

"You could ask."

The thought had never crossed her mind.

"What kind of amateur sleuth are you if you don't ask these things when you can?"

"I'm not an amateur sleuth and you are only one because you're . . ."

"I'm what?" Edie's voice turned dark.

"I think maybe Blue Sky is a little . . . tame for you after your time in the big city." The minute the words left her mouth she regretted them.

"What's that supposed to mean?"

"Nothing."

Edie pressed her lips together and seemed as if she was about to comment further, but someone cut her off as she turned into the hospital parking lot. She pressed the horn

— hard — and shouted "idiot!" at the guy and the moment was lost.

Thank you, Lord.

The last thing Kappy wanted was for Edie to realize that her life was boring and moving back to the city might be the answer. Maybe for Edie, but definitely not for Kappy and Jimmy.

"When we get up to the floor that her room is on, keep your ears open," Edie instructed.

"Is that possible?" Kappy had no idea. Maybe she should get a calendar with unbelievable actions on it. If she was going to hang around with Edie Peachey, that might not be a bad idea.

"Just listen. Someone may say something incriminating."

That wasn't a word on her calendar, but she could figure out what it meant. "*Jah.* Fine," she said, even though the whole idea was ridiculous. She should be at home, sewing, instead of out trying to solve a crime that she had no business nosing into. But the main thing was to keep Edie happy. Kappy could sacrifice an hour in order to keep her friend from leaving town once again.

"I wonder if anyone has taken into consideration that Alma might not be able to remember anything once she wakes up," Kappy mused as they stepped into the elevator to go up.

Edie swung around to face her, eyes wide. "I hadn't. But you're right. She might not be able to remember so much as her name."

"I didn't mean that. Isn't it possible that she might not be able to remember anything about the attack?"

"It's totally possible." Edie shook her head. "Why didn't I think of that before?"

"Of what?" The elevator dinged, and the door slid open. Kappy and Edie stepped out onto the seventh floor.

Edie bent down, nearly whispering in Kappy's ear as they turned toward the waiting area. "She might have total amnesia. But the attacker doesn't know that. If he wants her dead . . ." She trailed off with a suggestive lift of her eyebrows.

"Stop it." Kappy shooed her away. "We don't know anything of the sort."

"What else can it be?" Edie asked.

"Well it's certainly not a robbery gone bad if nothing was missing from the house."

"We don't know that for certain," Kappy protested, then cut her words short as they approached where the loved ones waited for news.

Bishop Sam sat with Preacher Sam on one

side of him and James Troyer, the deacon, on the other side. All three men sat with their heads bowed as if they had been sitting there all night, praying. Kappy figured that it was as likely as any other theory.

Kappy stopped in front of the bishop, searching for the words to ease his pain. She knew for a fact that Samuel Miller was a firm believer in God's will. He had preached about it enough that everyone in the district knew as well, but it didn't stop him from being worried about his wife. And for all his bluster and swagger, she could tell that he loved Alma very much.

He looked up, eyes dry, mouth pulled into a pinched smile of welcome. "Thank you for coming, Kappy." He reached out a hand. She took it, and he squeezed her fingers as if needing the touch to remind him that things would be the way they were supposed to be. Just human contact to say that he wasn't in this alone.

"Has there been any change?" Kappy asked. As she did, Edie moved around her and went to the other side of the bank of chairs. They were set up back to back in rows that faced the wall of the small area. If they sat there, they would be directly behind the bishop and the other church members. The men wouldn't be able to see them, but

Edie would be able to hear anything they said.

"No. But God willing, the nurses and doctors seem hopeful."

"That she'll be able to come home soon?"

He shrugged. "It's hard to say. She took quite a blow." Tear filled his eyes.

"An iron skillet doesn't have very many forgiving points," Preacher Sam added.

An iron skillet?

Kappy gave a little cough. Behind the bishop, Edie's mouth was hanging open. *Iron skillet?* she mouthed.

"She was . . . hit with a skillet?" Kappy asked.

"Cast iron," James Troyer added. "It's a shame that a woman can't cook safely in her own home these days. Something needs to be done."

"Amen," Edie replied, but not one of the men acknowledged her words. She rolled her eyes and plopped down behind James.

"Something will be done," Preacher Sam stated emphatically. "Just as soon as we get Alma well and back home."

"And we will," Kappy said, wondering how she got to be a part of the *we.* She lived just on the outside of everyone else. But she supposed tragedy brought all different kinds together. Even all different kinds of Amish.

"God willing," Bishop Sam said.

"God willing," the other two men echoed.

Kappy murmured something that she hoped sounded supportive, then tugged her fingers from the bishop's grasp. She cast one more glance at Bishop Sam, then followed Edie to the back side of the row. They sat down, their backs to the men, and began to wait.

As far as Kappy could tell, this was an utter waste of time. But she supposed that if Edie felt like she was doing something to help solve this enormous crime she had invented, then Kappy sitting and staring at the weird painting of a flower on the wall across from her was better than Edie running all over the valley accusing people of all sorts of crimes. Or simply leaving Blue Sky altogether.

"Ears open," Edie leaned close and whispered.

Not knowing how else to indicate that she was listening and her ears were indeed open, Kappy pretended to open her ears using imaginary keys.

Edie rolled her eyes and reached for a magazine. It was more than a little rough around the edges. Half of the title was missing, but there was enough of the cover left for Kappy to realize that it was about race cars. Without a hesitation, Edie opened the magazine and buried her nose in the pages.

Across the room someone coughed but since they had their backs to everyone in the room, Kappy didn't know if it was Englisher or Amish.

She glanced over to Edie, but her friend seemed to have fallen head first into the car magazine. How long were they going to sit here . . . doing . . . nothing . . . ? Had she really thought this was worth keeping Edie in town? Maybe she should have brought a pen and paper. She could have started a grocery list. Did she let Elmer out before they left?

Of course she did. She wouldn't have left him in the house.

But did she lock the yard gate? The last thing she needed was Elmer out roaming the countryside.

If she was being fair, he was a good dog, but he was still a dog — into everything, romping places he shouldn't go, and otherwise terrorizing small animals and plants that happened to get in his path. This summer she'd had a few problems keeping him in the yard and away from her neighbor's chickens and gladiolas. She hadn't had any problems since she, Edie, and Jimmy had gone to the hardware store and bought a new fence. Jack Jones had helped with the install and so far everything had worked just fine, keeping Elmer safely in the yard. Well, when she made sure the gate was locked.

As if thinking his name had conjured him from thin air, Jack Jones suddenly appeared in front of them. Edie jumped, obviously startled by his sudden appearance.

"What a surprise," Jones said. His eyes held a light that said their presence there was anything but a surprise. What a shock that Edie was on the heels of the next big crime in Kish Valley.

"Jack Jones." Edie recovered quickly, looking him up and down as if he were a bushel of vegetables she was about to buy.

"Edie." He nodded. "Is your hair . . . never mind." He shook his head, then frowned as if he'd made himself a little dizzy.

"What brings you here?" Edie asked.

"I think that's my question."

Edie stood and grabbed Jones by the arm, dragging him to the far corner of the waiting area, where no one waited. Kappy had no choice but to stand and follow behind them. Well, if she wanted to hear what they were saying.

Edie jerked a thumb in Kappy's direction. "My friend is worried about the bishop's wife. Alma is much loved around here."

It was true. There wasn't a soul who would wish Alma harm. Except for maybe Frannie Lehman. But their beef was about pie. And pie wasn't worth a skillet to the head . . . was it?

"No." Kappy didn't realize that she had said the word out loud until both Jack and Edie turned to her.

"What?" Edie asked.

"Nothing." Kappy waved it all away with the flick of one hand.

"And you are here because . . . ?" Edie asked Jack.

"I'm a cop."

"Don't you work homicide?" Edie continued.

"Usually, but Costas was out for the day and it landed on my desk."

"So you are working the case?" Kappy asked.

"Just for one more day," he explained.

"And why are you here again?" Edie wanted to know.

"To check on Alma. Gather what information I can before the trail gets cold. Costas will take over tomorrow."

"The investigation?" Edie quizzed.

"What else?"

"Because it's not a homicide?" she pressed

for clarification. "And you only handle homicides?"

"I think we already covered this part." He looked to Kappy for backup. She merely shrugged. He was on his own as far as she was concerned.

"I think she wants you to say whether or not you believe Alma will pull through," Kappy finally said.

"I have no idea. That's not my department."

"But homicide is," Edie threw in.

Jack turned to Kappy. "Does she have an off switch?"

"I wish," Kappy replied.

"I heard that," Edie grumbled.

"Then hear this," Jack Jones said. "Go home. You're not here to check on Alma. You're snooping around, trying to see if you can solve who attacked her."

"Aha." Edie raised one finger into the air, a triumphant gesture. "So there is a case."

Jack just shook his head and started down the hall toward the nurses' station.

CHAPTER 4

"I am so disappointed in Jack," Edie said as they headed across the parking lot toward her car.

As far as Kappy was concerned, that was one wasted hour. They had gone to the hospital to get some sort of idea about what happened to Alma and why, but they were no more enlightened than when they arrived. Except for the part about the skillet.

"Uh-huh," Kappy murmured, hoping the sound would soothe Edie enough that she could let it go.

No such luck.

"I am just so disappointed in him."

"I believe you've said that before."

Edie gave a low growl of frustration as she unlocked the car and pulled her door open. "I mean, really. Worried about semantics when the poor bishop's wife is near death."

Once again Kappy was grateful for her word-a-day calendar. She knew what *seman-*

tics meant. But the part about Alma being near death . . . well, that was something she didn't understand at all.

As far as she knew, Alma was in bad shape, but was being allowed time to rest and heal before they woke her. She was not in good health by any stretch nor was she knocking on heaven's gates.

But after one look at Edie's face, she thought better of pointing that out to her. Kappy got into the car and buckled her seat belt and Edie eased out of her spot. After a few moments of silence, they pulled out onto the main road and headed toward Mose Peachey's bait shop.

"Like really . . . did you believe that story about him being there because the detective who was supposed to take the case was out?"

Kappy shrugged. She opened her mouth to answer, but Edie plowed on.

"It's nonsense that's what it is. Alma has to be much worse off or she wouldn't be in any kind of coma, you know what I mean?"

"Well —"

"And he expects us to believe it. Whatever."

Kappy relaxed back into her seat, as much as she could, what with the way Edie was driving. Kappy supposed it wasn't *bad* driving, but it was unnerving to her. Even after several months of riding around in Edie's car, Kappy hadn't gotten used to Edie's distracted driving style and moving at such a quick pace. It was . . . well, unnerving. And too quick. She much preferred buggy travel. But at any rate, Edie might be talking *at* her, but she wasn't talking *with* her and had no need of Kappy's responses. She was almost used to it now. Instead, she tried her best not to clutch the dash and held on while Edie ranted.

Before long, they pulled into the parking lot at the bait shop.

"There is only one reason why he was there," Edie continued. "He believes Alma is going to die. They must all believe that."

"You don't know that," Kappy protested.

"I do."

"But the doctors all said —"

"Mark my words." Edie stabbed the air with one finger. "Alma is on her way out. And there's nothing anyone can do about it."

Kappy wanted to protest, but before she could so much as gather her thoughts, Jimmy came bounding out of the shop, the grin on his face stretching completely across.

"Hey, Edie. Hey, Kappy." He slid into the

73

back seat, oblivious of the tension that hovered in the car. "We're going, right?"

"Going where?" Kappy asked.

"To enter me in the small animal competition at the festival."

Edie groaned. "Can we do it later?"

"No." Jimmy frowned. "Today is the last day to register for the animals. If I don't do it now . . ."

His sister laid her forehead against the steering wheel.

"Edie?" he asked, concern tinging his voice. "Are you okay?"

She sighed and raised her head. Kappy patted her on the shoulder.

"I'm fine," she said. Though Kappy had a feeling she would rather go back to the hospital and see if she could track down Alma's doctors.

That was the thing about boredom, it would make a person do all sorts of wacky things. Edie was nothing if not bored. But maybe if Kappy could keep her busy and out of Jack Jones's way, she would be able to occupy her time and not put his investigation in jeopardy.

"Are we going?" Jimmy bounced up and down in the back seat. "Please, Edie. I want to do this so badly."

She nodded and put the car in gear. "I

know, buddy. I know." She pulled the car out of the parking lot and headed toward downtown and the village council offices.

Kappy could tell that Edie still wasn't convinced that allowing Jimmy to enter was a good idea, but she went along with it anyway. It wasn't the entry fee or the thought of competition, but she was worried about Jimmy's well-being mentally if he didn't win. Kappy knew that he could handle it.

They parked the car in the first available spot, then the three of them made their way into the council building.

Kappy had only been inside the building a couple of times, but she remembered where a couple of the offices were located. The person in charge of licensing and grants was to the left and all the way down the hall. "This way," she said, pointing in the right direction. Edie and Jimmy followed her down the well-lit hallway. The walls were painted a soothing cream color above the oak chair rail and a deep burgundy below. Somehow it worked with the light brown carpet and framed photos on the wall. Kappy studied these as she walked, not taking too much time, but doing her best to see what they were all about. Most were shots of past festivals. They appeared to be taken by a professional photographer, most likely one of the winners of the previous photo contests that were a part of the festival each year.

"Here." She stopped in front of the last door, reaching out a hand to open it.

Edie captured her fingers in a firm grip. "Hold on." Not releasing Kappy's hand, she turned back to her brother. "Are you sure you want to do this?"

"Yes, Edie." Jimmy could barely keep the aggravation from his voice. Yet he still sounded like the frustrated young man he was.

"I'm just making sure," she said, her tone growing defensive.

"E-die," he groaned.

Edie let go of Kappy's hand and together they walked into the licensing office.

Inside was more of the same from the hallway. Half-cream-half-burgundy-colored walls. More photographs of festivals past. Except for one wall. It was covered with plaques. Large ones that had many little brass plates just big enough for one person's name. Some of the plaques were completely filled with the small brass strips, while others it seemed had places just waiting for new names.

Edie approached the desk and started to

explain to the receptionist what she and Jimmy were after. Kappy eased toward the award wall, strangely interested in the names she would find there.

Of course not many of the names were ones she recognized. Especially on the plaques dedicated to the more English pursuits like photography and art. But there were several names she knew on the quilting plaque and of course Alma's name dominated the pie-baking contest. She had won for the last seven years and even before that, Frannie Lehman wasn't among the list of winners.

Suddenly, Kappy was filled with sadness for the woman. How terrible to have such a dream and not be able to realize it. Everyone in the district knew that Frannie's biggest wish in life was to beat Alma just once, even one time, and Kappy knew Frannie would be a changed person. At least she probably wouldn't look like she had swallowed a rotten persimmon all the time. And that would be an improvement.

"About the pie contest," Kappy heard Edie say. "I read something the other day that said all the contestants are baking the same kind of pie this year."

"That's right." The woman who sat behind the glass partition had a long brown ponytail and a sweet smile. "Would you like an entry form for the pie competition?" She made to get one out of her filing cabinet, but Edie stopped her just in time.

"No. No. That's okay." Edie's voice was rushed. "I just thought it was interesting that the rules had changed."

The receptionist looked first one way and then the other as if checking to see if anyone could overhear. As far as Kappy could tell, they were alone in the office, but who knew what went on inside that glass box. Or even behind it.

The girl's eyes twinkled as she leaned forward. "One of the contestants from last year complained that it wasn't fair when two different pies were pitted against one another. The council mulled it over and decided that she might have something."

"Really?" Edie's voice was almost a gush. She was certainly turning on the charm to get information from the girl behind the counter.

The girl nodded, her ponytail swishing with the motion.

"But who would do such a thing?" Edie asked.

Once again the receptionist looked both ways and back behind her. Then she leaned in so close, close enough that even if someone had been trying to overhear they wouldn't have been able to. "I'm not one hundred percent sure, but rumor around the office is Frannie Lehman."

"It's just a rumor." Kappy practically had to skip to keep up with Edie and her long purposeful strides. She had an agenda. Now if only Kappy knew what it was.

"Where are we going?" she asked as she got into the car.

Edie shrugged. "Home, I guess."

"*Jah,* I want to start preparing Judith Junior for the competition." Jimmy clapped his hands together.

Edie started the car and whipped it toward the parking lot exit lane. The tires squealed in protest as she zipped out on the main road.

"Quit driving so fast," Kappy complained.

Edie immediately took her foot off the gas pedal, but she sighed as she did so.

"I wonder what kind of pie it is," Jimmy mused.

"What?" Edie sat up a little in her seat so she could peer at Jimmy in the rearview mirror.

"The lady said the pie bakers are baking only one kind of pie. I wonder what kind."

"What kind . . . ?" Edie mused settling

back into her seat. "Oh, gosh! That could be the answer."

"What?" Kappy asked. Sometimes Edie's brain moved way too fast and Kappy could not keep up with her thoughts.

"The pie." Edie slowed the car, swung it onto a side road, then went back the way they just came.

"What are you doing?" Kappy asked.

"I'm going back to talk to the ponytail girl."

"Why?"

"I like her," Jimmy said from the back seat. "She was nice. And pretty."

"So she can tell me what kind of pie they're baking for the competition."

Kappy grabbed the dash as Edie swung around a slower moving car. "There are buggies on this road, too, you know."

"I know." She eased up on the gas a little but didn't really slow down.

"The pie will still be the same if you get it in five minutes or ten."

Her words seemed to hit home with Edie. She actually used the brake to slow the car to the speed limit. "I get it," Edie grumbled. "I make you nervous when I drive."

"I'm not nervous," Jimmy chimed in.

"Well, that's because you are entirely too trusting," Kappy said.

"But you love me for it." Jimmy grinned.

"You got that right."

Thankfully, her exchange with Jimmy calmed Kappy just a bit and soon they were once again pulling into the parking lot at the council building.

Edie found a spot and shut off the car in record time. Before Kappy even got her seat belt unfastened, Edie was out of the car and on her way to the building.

"Why are you in such a hurry?" she asked.

"We don't have all day." But Edie stopped, allowing Jimmy and Kappy to bridge half the distance that separated them.

"We sort of do," Kappy returned.

"No, really," Jimmy said. "I have to feed the animals around four or they'll get too hungry and that is not a good thing."

"First you criticize my driving, now I'm walking too fast." Edie waved a hand behind her, then pushed her way into the building.

Kappy wasn't sure if the wave was a dismissal or an apology. At any rate, she and Jimmy followed behind.

"I just love your hair," the woman behind the glass window was saying when they approached. "I wanted to tell you when you were here, but I didn't have the chance."

"Thank you," Edie said impatiently. "Can you tell me what kind of pie the ladies will have to bake for the competition?"

"We allow men to bake, too, you know." Though Kappy had never seen even one male entrant in the bake off. That was something she felt she would have noticed. "We're progressive that way."

"Good for you." Edie strummed her fingers impatiently on the counter.

Ponytail just stared at her blankly.

"The pie?" Edie asked.

"Oh, yes. Are you thinking about entering?"

"No," Kappy said, but her words crashed with Edie's "yes."

"Maybe," Edie said by way of recovery.

"That'll be great," Ponytail gushed.

Edie continued to strum.

"Right." The girl stood and made her way over to a bank of filing cabinets. There was a row of them, six in all, and Kappy wondered just how many papers the council had that needed to be filed. Or how the girl knew which one of the many drawers housed the papers she needed. Somehow she did. She opened a drawer, rifled through the folders, and triumphantly produced a file. She took a paper from the inside and handed it to Edie. "Would you like one, too?" she asked Kappy.

Edie didn't seem to be too keen on sharing, so Kappy nodded and took the paper from Ponytail.

"Thank you," she said, but her gaze was already centered on the page.

"Are you kidding me?" Edie's tone was near a screech. "Boysenberry? The pie for this year is boysenberry?"

Ponytail nodded, her mouth pulled into a serious angle. "It says on the back how the type of pie was chosen and what the other varieties were in the mix. It was all done above board and completely monitored by an outside source."

"An outside source?" Edie pinned the girl with a sharp look. "Who?"

"That nice detective at the sheriff's office, Jack Jones."

"I can't believe it," Edie said as she slid behind the wheel of her car. "He knew all along."

Kappy fastened her seat belt. "He knew what all along?"

"That the pie was going to be boysenberry. That's why he was at the hospital."

"That doesn't make any sense, Edie. Why would boysenberry pie draw Jack Jones to the hospital?"

"Because he knew that Alma's attack was intentional."

"Of course he did. Everyone did."

"But Jack knew it was about pie."

Kappy shook her head. "It can't be about pie."

"Why not?"

"Because it can't be."

Edie didn't seem convinced. "You thought Sally June's death wasn't about pickles, either."

Kappy shot her a look. But Edie wasn't fazed. For once she was paying attention to her driving. "People do crazy things for crazy reasons."

"This is a little too crazy."

"Sounds crazy to me," Jimmy said, not wanting to be left out of the conversation.

"Think about it. Frannie Lehman has spent most of her adult life building her bakery into something noteworthy."

"How do you know all of this?" Kappy asked. "You weren't even here when her husband died."

Edie gave a quick shrug. "Being shunned has it benefits. When people pretend that you're not there, eventually they come to believe it themselves and will say a lot of things they may not have said in front of you before."

Kappy turned that one over in her mind until she could make sense of it. "So you've been eavesdropping?"

"I prefer to think of it as recon."

That word definitely was not on her calendar.

"Seriously, though," Edie continued. "Frannie does all this hard work to make ends meet with a baby and so many small children and she can't beat Alma's boysenberry pie. Not even with her own best recipe."

"So you think Frannie was the one who attacked Alma?" Kappy shook her head, trying to wrap her mind around that one.

"Who else?"

"A robber."

Edie shook her head. "Seventy-five percent of people who are attacked are attacked by someone they know."

"You just made that up," Kappy said calmly.

"Maybe, but you know it's true. Most crimes like this aren't random. You've seen *NCIS*. No, wait, you haven't. Scratch that. Everyone with a television set knows it's true."

Kappy shot her a look. "I don't have a TV set, so I'll have to take your word for it."

"Good girl."

They drove in silence for a moment.

"Do you really think Frannie would attack Alma over a pie recipe?"

"Stanger things have happened."

"Not in Blue Sky," Kappy countered.

"Then I suppose we're due."

"That's not true, either," Kappy said, but the thought had the hairs on her arms sticking up.

"Shouldn't we tell all this to Jack?" Jimmy asked.

"The voice of reason." Kappy shot Edie a look, but once again she was paying attention to her driving. Go figure.

"We don't have anything to tell Jack," Edie stated.

"We can tell him about the pies."

Edie shook her head. "That's not really something."

Kappy looked over one shoulder. A frown creased Jimmy's brow and his head was cocked to one side as if he was thinking about something. Hard. "It seemed to be a few minutes ago."

Edie scoffed. "No." But she made the word so long no one believed her.

"We could invite him over for supper," Jimmy continued, "and maybe he will bring another one of those cakes." Jimmy rubbed his tummy and licked his lips. "Yum-my."

"We are not inviting Jack Jones over, and he is not bringing a cake he probably bought at the store anyway."

Kappy thought back to the beautiful lemon cake Jack had brought over the last time he had eaten with the three of them. True, the cake looked almost too perfect to eat and seemed more like a bakery purchase than the efforts of a bachelor cop. But Kappy knew people well enough to know that anything was possible. Yet the thought of Jack in an apron with a smear of flour on his face was almost more than she could stand. Dark and brooding, Jack Jones was certainly not the baking type.

"Now I want cake," Kappy grumbled.

"Me, too," Jimmy chirped from the back seat.

"Well, you're in luck," Edie said, switching on her blinker so she could turn the car around. "I happen to know the best place in town to get cake."

CHAPTER 5

"You did this on purpose," Kappy accused as she got out of the car.

"You said you wanted cake." Edie gave a quick shrug of one shoulder and turned to the large white sign that professed their destination. **FRANNIE'S BAKERY,** the sign declared in big black letters, and underneath was written: CAKES, PIES, WHOOPIE PIES, PASTRIES, AND MORE.

"Yay," Jimmy cried. "Cake!"

Together they made their way toward the steps leading down into Frannie Lehman's basement bakery.

Kappy had been to Frannie's several times but it had been a while. As was usual, some things were perfectly the same while others had changed. The sign at the cash register asking for ones and fives was the same one that had always been there. The proof was in the tattered corners and random marks where people had tried to get a pen writing again. The previous display cases had been replaced with ones that looked older in style but were too perfect to be anything but replicas. To Kappy, they resembled old deli counters with large windows to display the meat. Or in this case, the cookies, pies, and treats. The place was still lit by only the screen-covered windows that lined the walls just below the ceiling.

"I love this place." Jimmy rubbed his hands together, his gaze firmly fixed on the display cabinets filled with goodies.

"He's not the only one," Edie said in a low voice for only Kappy to hear.

It was true. Frannie's was hopping and business had to be good.

Kappy took a moment to scan the workers behind the counter. Three women besides Frannie herself kneaded dough, wielded icing bags, and monitored the large ovens. Kappy recognized them at once. Amanda Lehman and Susie Lehman were Frannie's two eldest daughters, while Rosie M was married to Danny Lehman, Frannie's oldest child and only son.

He had been young when his father died. Eleven or twelve, Kappy couldn't remember. But time moved on and he was now married. And with his own family on the way, she noted, taking one look at the rounded belly of Rosie M.

"What are we looking for?" Kappy asked in a low voice.

Edie gave her the most innocent look. "Cake, of course." But she headed over to the pie counter.

Kappy dutifully followed behind.

The pies on display were beautiful. Not in that store-bought perfect way, but in the yummy, I-can't-wait-to-eat-you way. All were golden brown with rustic edges that Kappy had heard referred to as artisan. Whatever it was, it made the pies look both delicious and handmade. Both of which were good qualities for pies.

"Apple, cherry, boysenberry," Edie murmured, almost but not quite dragging one finger along the glass case in front of her. "What the heck is a boysenberry anyway?"

"It's a hybrid between a European raspberry and blackberry, an American dewberry, and I believe a loganberry."

Edie rolled her eyes. "How do you even know that?"

"The library, I guess . . . seed catalog." She shrugged. Who knew? "Alma's favorite pie to make," Kappy mused.

"And Frannie prefers the crab apple." Kappy shot her a look. "Or so I hear." Edie shrugged. "So is Frannie's crab apple pie

90

better than Alma's boysenberry?"

"Not in the last seven years."

Edie laughed. Once again Alma's pies reigned supreme.

"Ew," Jimmy said from behind them. "Pumpkin pie."

Kappy shook her head. "What about sweet potato pie?" she asked.

"Vegetable," Jimmy chimed.

"You need to eat more fruits and vegetables," Edie grumbled, picking that moment to be parent of the year.

"I don't like their colors." Jimmy shivered as if a cold wind blew on him and him alone.

"But they are also crunchy," Kappy pointed out. "And if you close your eyes, you don't know what color they are."

He seemed to think that over for a moment and not having a good answer, he moved toward the section set up for cookies.

"One day," Edie promised as he walked away.

"Uh-huh," Kappy agreed, though she didn't know if Edie would ever be successful at overcoming Jimmy's food-color issues. He hated all red food, preferring to eat beige and tan. Like . . .

"Oh." He sighed. "Peanut butter cookies."

Like peanut butter cookies.

Edie all but turned in a circle, as if taking in all the details of the bakery. "She's doing good for herself," she muttered. "Kappy, how much is the prize money for the bake off?"

"The paper said three hundred dollars."

"Three hundred dollars. Hmm . . ."

"I don't think that's enough motivation given the business we see here." There was no way. And if Frannie had somehow run into some trouble of some sort, three hundred dollars didn't sound like enough to make a difference.

"Maybe it's pride," Edie countered.

"Pride is a sin and we do our best to avoid its clutches."

"Then why bother having a competition at all?"

Kappy opened her mouth to respond, then thought better of it and closed it again.

"Oh, look," Edie cried. "Donuts. We have to get some for Jack."

"I still don't understand the joke about cops and donuts," Kappy said a while later as they rode in Edie's car to the sheriff's office.

"It's like cops eat donuts instead of — You know what? Never mind. I just hope he likes maple cream."

"And these donuts are going to give us a way to know the real reason Alma was hit on the head and left . . . on her kitchen floor." She had almost said *left to die,* but she was worried how Jimmy would take it. His own mother had been found much the same way, except she had been attacked in their barn.

"It's okay," Jimmy said from the back seat. "You can say what you really want to say. I'm a man now, and I can hear it."

He might be a man in body, but in mind and spirit he was still something of a child. A sweet wonderful child. But a child all the same. But Kappy could tell; Jimmy was ready to move on a bit. All this talk about food and raising pigs. She was waiting on the day for him to ask for even bigger animals. And to drive. It was only a matter of time before Jimmy wanted free rein to drive all around the valley. She just wasn't sure what Edie would think of that.

"I know, Jimmy," Kappy said and lifted a hand over the back of the seat. He squeezed her fingers in a reassuring way. All was well.

Edie turned her car into the parking lot at the sheriff's office and parked in the nearest space she could find. Several other cars were parked there along with a few patrol vehicles complete with lights all the way across the top.

"I hope he's here," Kappy muttered as she got out of the car.

"I like Jack," Jimmy said.

"We know," Edie groaned.

"Well, I do," Jimmy said with a huff.

"I do, too." Kappy nodded her head in firm agreement.

Edie stopped. "You like Jack?"

"Of course I do. But not like that."

Edie pressed a hand to her heart. "Scared me there for a minute. I thought you were about to jump the fence."

"Hardly."

"If you jump the fence, who will make all the coverings for the women? That's what Martha Peachey always says." Jimmy shot them a mischievous grin. Martha had been convinced as long as Kappy could remember that she, Kappy, would leave the Amish, forcing all the women in the area to go around with their heads uncovered. Like that would ever happen. Kappy wasn't going to leave Blue Sky, but if she did, the women would find someone to make their *kapps.* Or wear bandanas at the very least.

But more than that, Jimmy's words told her just how much of the conversations around him he heard when other people thought he wasn't listening.

"Come on." Edie hooked one arm toward the brick building, then stopped as the man they were there to see stepped outside. "Well, as I live and breathe, Jack Jones." Edie's accent was horribly Southern, completely over the top, and dripping with sugar.

Kappy shook her head and covered her eyes with her fingers. Edie had to stop watching that television show *Designing Women.* Kappy wasn't sure what they designed only that they designed something and drew out their words until they were twice as long as they needed to be. Edie said it wasn't that she so much liked the show, but she had limited access to television since she had to watch everything on her phone. To Kappy, that sounded like something straight out of the future, so she supposed she would watch a show she didn't care for just to see the miracle.

"Edith Peachey. I told you that I am not on the case and neither should you be."

Edie frowned, but the action looked theatrical. Kappy wasn't sure where she had heard that word, but it wasn't from her calendar. At any rate, it fit.

"I come bearing gifts," Edie said, holding up the pastry box from Frannie's.

"Trojan horse?" Jack asked.

"Don't look a gift horse," Edie returned.

Kappy wasn't sure what any of this had to do with horses, but with the time that Edie had spent with the English, she understood that her friend had walked a very different path.

"And don't call me, Edith, Jack-o'-lantern."

"Jack-o'-lantern," Jimmy echoed. "That's funny."

"Only if it's not your name," Jack said.

"Your name isn't Jack-o'-lantern?" Edie's eyes grew wide enough that Kappy knew that she was teasing him. Maybe even flirting with him . . .

"What can I do for you today?"

"I told you. I brought you a gift." She offered it to him once again.

Jack looked down into the clear cellophane window in the top of the box. "Donuts?"

"Funny, right?"

"Not so much."

"You don't have to take them." Edie reached toward the box.

"Are these maple creams from Frannie's?"

"Sure are."

"Then I accept. But I have to ask what you were doing at Frannie's."

"Buying donuts." Edie flipped her hair over her shoulder, which was quite a feat since it barely reached it.

"No," Jimmy protested. "We went to get cake. Remember? You said —"

Edie pressed her fingers to his lips. "We'll get a cake later."

Jimmy stopped talking and Edie turned back to Jones.

Kappy just watched, taking it all in. This was almost as good as that comedy skit about baseball she had seen once as a kid. Almost.

"He just loves that lemon cake you brought for dinner a while back. He can't stop talking about it, so I took him to Frannie's to see if that's where you got it."

Surprised was a mild word for what Kappy felt as she spied the stain of red rising up under the collar of Jack Jones's crisp blue dress shirt. It seeped into his stubbly cheeks and made its way clear up to his forehead, just under where his jet-black hair started. "No, I didn't get it at Frannie's."

"Then where did —"

Jack appeared to be very uncomfortable, an unusual look for him. "Can we talk about this some other time?"

"Well, really I came to ask you about Alma."

"Is it just me or is anyone else experiencing déjà vu?"

"Of course not," Edie scoffed playfully.

"So we didn't have this exact same conversation this morning at the hospital?"

Edie laughed, but the sound came out sort of choked. "No."

"Sure seems like it." He rubbed his chin, his palm against the short beard growth making a rasping sound.

"Well, it's not, because this morning I didn't bring you donuts and I didn't ask you to come to dinner tomorrow."

"Like a date?"

It was Edie's turn to become the color of pickled beets. "Just friends. We're all friends, right?" She swept one arm about as if encompassing them all.

"Sure."

"Don't forget to bring cake," Jimmy chimed in.

"It'll give us a chance to catch up."

Jack smiled. "And you can tell me all about what you've found out during your snooping trips."

"That man," Edie fumed as they drove home. "He wants to know what I know *and* he took the donuts."

"In all fairness, you did offer them as a

gift," Kappy said. "And you probably should tell him what we know."

"We don't know anything,"

"We know about the pie contest. Isn't that a clue?"

"Of course it's a clue, but that doesn't mean I want to tell him. I mean, it's not like it's a big secret. He helped them choose the pie."

"But he doesn't know that we know."

"The announcement was probably in the paper," Edie grumbled.

"I read the paper every morning."

"Perhaps you missed it, then."

"Maybe," Kappy murmured. It was possible, she supposed. Or that she read it and forgot it since it hadn't pertained to her at the time. "We should still tell Jack."

"Maybe I will."

Kappy shook her head. "That's not what I meant." But she knew Edie; once she had a plan in her head, right or wrong, good or bad, she was going to see it through. It was both a strength and a weakness.

Edie pulled down School Yard Road and right past Kappy's house. She supposed that it was simply habit. And she really didn't mind. Elmer was in the backyard playing and enjoying the beautiful day. He didn't have to be fed until later, so she could spend a little more time with Edie and Jimmy.

The dogs barked like mad as they got out of the car. It was different than a *there's a stranger* bark. More of a *thank heavens you're home come play* sort of bark. And these days that noise was joined with the bleating of Jimmy's new goats. Edie had bought him two and hadn't asked if they were male or female. She got one of each and now Jimmy was going to get a new goat in a couple of months.

"See over there." Jimmy pointed to a flat section of land on the far side of the dog pens. The dogs had quieted down a bit, but he still had to raise his voice to be heard. "That's where I want to put the pigpen."

Edie groaned loud enough to be heard over the puppy raucous. "Jimmy, I haven't agreed to pigs."

"You did," he protested, and for a moment Kappy was certain that he was about to stomp his foot on the ground in a temper tantrum. She had seen that once before, but he had been much younger.

"Jimmy." Edie raised one brow in what Kappy had come to call her *that's final* look.

"You did," Jimmy continued.

"I don't want to have this argument." She locked the car and headed for the house, Jimmy right on her heels.

"You told me I could get goats and pigs."

"You got goats." She let them into the house. Kappy followed.

"But you said pigs, too."

"Pigs smell."

"Then let's get the little kind. The ones you can keep in the house like Chris Esh has. They don't smell."

"And they are very expensive."

"You just don't want me to have them." Jimmy crossed his arms over his chest and stared at his sister. "But I'm grown now. I have a job, and I have my own money. I'll just save for a pig."

"Fine," Edie said, shocking Kappy. Was this all about money?

"Fine." Jimmy nodded.

"Get one of the outside ones and when it gets big enough, we'll eat it."

Jimmy faltered a bit, then regained his verbal footing. "You did promise me," he said, then turned for the stairs. "And *Mamm* said you should never break a promise."

Edie didn't respond; she just watched as Jimmy opened the door to his room and disappeared inside.

"I did no such thing," she said and looked to Kappy for confirmation.

Kappy winced. "I'm not sure what conversation you're remembering, but the one I heard . . . you promised him pigs."

Kappy spent the following morning working on her special orders. All that she had waiting were from women she had sewn for before and she had their patterns on hand. Then it just became a matter of cutting out the fabric, carefully stitching it together, and sewing on the strings. It sounded easy enough, but it took time and care to make the *kapps* according to the standard of the district. But Kappy loved her job. She loved taking small pieces of sheer white organdy and sewing them together. She liked taking something that could be anything and making it into a sacred piece of an Amish woman's daily life. She shouldn't gain so much satisfaction from her job, but she did. She was certain this love she felt was something akin to pride, vanity, or arrogance. Maybe even all three. So after she sewed, she prayed that she had done what God had wanted of her, and she did it with the grace and love He expected. That was how Aunt Hettie did it and that was how Kappy did it, too.

She had just finished the second *kapp* of the day when Elmer jumped to his feet and barked all the way to the door. His tail was wagging the entire time, so Kappy knew the person on the other side was friend not foe.

Then she opened the door to find Hiram Lapp standing there.

"Hi-Hiram," she sputtered. She shook her head and pushed Elmer back from the threshold with one foot.

"Hi, Kappy. Can I come in?"

There was no reason for him not to other than they had broken up and he had no reason to be at her house. No reason at all.

"Uh, no. I mean, yes." She stood to the side still blocking Elmer as Hiram stepped inside.

Once upon a time, she and Hiram had been something of a thing. But looking back on it now, she realized that it was a bigger thing to her than it had been to him. But there had been a time . . .

"It's good to see you." He took off his hat and twirled it in his hands.

"You, too."

He nodded as Elmer continued to race around him, doing everything in his puppy power to get the man to pay attention to him. Hiram ignored him.

Hiram hates dogs.

Edie's words echoed around in her head. That couldn't be true; nobody hated dogs. Hiram was just not as demonstrative as others in showing his love and appreciation for

God's wondrous creatures.

"May I sit down?" He gestured toward the couch.

Kappy nodded. Hiram sat, then patted the cushion next to him.

She ignored the gesture and sat in the rocker instead. She could always say that she normally sat there and so she did it out of habit, but she didn't want to sit next to Hiram. There were so many times that he seemed to have some kind of power over her. Like he could make her feel, say, and think things that maybe weren't her own. She knew it was ridiculous but those were her feelings all the same.

Disappointment pulled at the corners of his mouth, but he corrected it easily and met her gaze across the corner of the rectangular coffee table. "I was in the neighborhood and thought I would stop in and see how you are. I haven't seen you in a while."

That was because she hadn't been in his store in a while. Sundries and Sweets sold just about everything a person could want right down to the hand-dipped chocolates Joan the Mennonite made. But Kappy had been avoiding going in there, or rather taking the chance that she might run into Hiram. Instead she had been making the longer trip to the Super Saver and getting everything she needed there. It would have made her mindful heart feel better to have bought from Hiram, a local business owner. But her girl heart knew that if she was going to make this breakup really work that she had to stay away until she stopped thinking about him completely. At least that's what she read in that woman's magazine at the grocery store. There were several other articles that she had stumbled upon, which she supposed somehow helped English women with their relationships. Being Amish, she thought it better to skip them altogether rather than risk not being able to redeem herself from their tawdry messages.

Tawdry. That was today's word. She knew she wouldn't have much use for it, so she was glad to get it in a sentence on the day it was given to her.

"Kappy?"

She raised her eyes, her gaze meeting Hiram's concerned one. She supposed she looked like someone people should be concerned about. She had been sitting in a rocking chair staring at nothing and smiling as if she had just been guaranteed a spot in heaven.

"I'm sorry, Hiram. What were you saying?"

"You were a million miles away."

"Not so far," she murmured.

"I said I hoped that you have had time to think about our relationship."

She shook her head. "We don't have a relationship."

"Of course we do." He reached for her hand, but she moved it out of reach, pretending to pet Elmer even though the puppy had settled down for a nap next to her rocking chair. She would have to remember not to lean back lest his tail get under one of the rockers. Like he kept his tail still that long. Even now as he lay on his side, eyes closed and breathing even, his tail was switching back and forth. To have that kind of continual joy. What a blessing!

"Okay, let me rephrase that. We don't have a romantic relationship. Not anymore."

His expression crumbled at her words. "I thought that if I gave you enough time . . . Who is it?"

"What?" Kappy frowned, not understanding one word of what he was asking.

"Who is it? If you are not going to marry me, then you must be courting someone else. Who is it?"

Silas Hershberger's face popped into her thoughts. She took a good imaginary look at his handsome features, dark hair, eyes

106

the color of the sky just before the stars completely took over. Even white teeth, dazzling smile. Yes, the man's smile was dazzling.

She pushed the image away. She wasn't courting Silas and she certainly wasn't going to marry him. She had thought there was a spark between them, but so far he hadn't asked her on any dates. He just always made it a point to talk to her after church. And that didn't mean they had any relationship other than a friendship.

"Who is it?" Hiram asked quietly.

She stopped smiling, only then realizing that she had been. "No one," she said. It was true and not all true at the same time.

"I thought we were going to take it slow," Kappy said.

Hiram nodded. It was indeed what they had said a few months ago. And since then, Kappy had been busy living her own life. She had made friends with Edie and deepened her friendship with Jimmy and somehow the importance of her relationship with Hiram had fallen behind. Maybe importance wasn't a word, but certainly the urgency was no longer there.

"I thought we were going to be friends," she said.

"That's what we said, and yet you and I

107

have a connection." He stopped, rubbed his chin. "It's Silas Hershberger, isn't it?"

Kappy froze even as a heat began to fill her. "There's no one. You and I need to take a break. Take things slowly. We rushed into everything way too fast. One minute we're burying your wife and my best friend and the next thing I know we're engaged." She shook her head. "I'm surprised the bishop even allowed it."

"He allowed it because he knows we belong together."

"Why are you in the neighborhood today?" She knew the answer but wanted him to say the words.

"I was running errands."

"You were at the cemetery."

His cheeks turned pink. "She was my wife."

"I know." And he loved her very much. More than he would ever love Kappy. "When you are truly over her death, maybe then . . ." She stood and gestured toward the door.

Hiram remained seated. "Let's talk about something else," he said.

"Hiram."

"*Mamm* isn't entering the pie bake off this year."

Kappy stopped. He was just trying to

extend their conversation. He just wanted to stay. She knew he hoped that by lingering he could change her mind, but she was stronger now than she had been after Laverna's death. She could be friends with Hiram and that might be all they could have between them. But friends could talk about the pie bake off, couldn't they?

She dropped back into her seat, one of the rockers pressing down on Elmer's tail. He was on his feet in a flash, yelping and biting at the invisible foe who had nipped his tail.

"Poor pooch." Kappy scooped him into her arms, kissing the top of his head.

The look of disgust on Hiram's face was almost priceless. She supposed he might hate dogs after all. What kind of person hated dogs?

"So why is your mother not entering the contest?" Elmer squirmed and Kappy set him on his feet. He ran toward the squeaky toy lying near the coatrack and proceeded to show it who was in charge.

"Haven't you heard? They are all baking the same pie this year. *Mamm* decided she hated her recipe for boysenberry pie and would never be able to win." He shrugged. "She didn't enter."

Kappy mulled that over for a moment.

"Why do you suppose they would change the contest like that this year?"

"It's been speculated that there will be a special judge this year and —" He stopped.

"Spill it," Kappy ordered.

"Some people are wondering if perhaps boysenberry was chosen so that Alma would be assured to win."

"Why would they want that?" Kappy asked more of herself than him. But Hiram answered anyway.

"Maybe because they think it'll put Blue Sky on the map."

"We're not on the map?"

"You know what I mean."

"So who is this special judge?" Maybe that was the key. Nothing else seemed to be fitting.

"Bobbie Jean Hawkins."

O-kay. "Who's Bobbie Jean Hawkins?"

"According to my mother who talked to Frannie who discussed it with Diana Chamberland —"

"The owner of Blue Sky Baked Goods?"

"The one and the same."

"Continue." She waved one hand in a circular motion as if that would get him started again. She had never met Diana Chamberland, but she had heard the woman was as old as the hills and could make a mean bear claw.

"So according to my sources, which also happens to be the underground railroad of gossip between the English and the Amish, she works for Mrs. O'Malley's Pies."

CHAPTER 6

"The question is," Edie said that evening as they put the finishing touches on their meal. "Why is an employee of one of the largest pastry companies in this area coming all the way here to judge our piddly contest?"

"I'm not sure Frannie and Alma consider it piddly." Kappy gave a small shrug and scooped out a sample bite of mashed potatoes to give them a quick taste. "Maybe this is part of her personal journey."

"Have you been reading self-help books again? I'm sure Bishop Sam would not approve." She cocked her head to one side. "Now who told you all this?"

Kappy nearly choked. She shoved another bite into her mouth and shrugged. "I just heard it around town," she mumbled around the food. "It might not even be true."

"You're right, of course," Edie agreed. "And stop eating the potatoes or there won't be any to serve when Jack gets here."

As if on cue, a knock sounded at the door.

Edie shook her head, her hands covered in flour. She had been kneading the rolls one last time. "I have got to get a doorbell," she muttered. "Jimmy! Door!"

"I can get it," Kappy said, drying her hands on the nearby dishtowel.

"Thanks. I need to get these in the oven. I forgot they took so long to make."

Kappy smiled. "Maybe you should cook more."

"Maybe you should answer the door like you said you would."

"I'm going. I'm going." She tossed the towel back onto the counter and made her way to the front of the house.

"Jack Jones," she greeted. "What brings you here?"

He cocked his head to the yard behind him. "My car. May I come in?"

She looked to the plastic container he carried. It was the right size and shape. "Is that cake?"

"It is."

"Then you may."

He chuckled as she stepped back and allowed him to enter.

Just then, Jimmy came bounding down the stairs, his emergency call necklace swinging around his neck. "Jack! You're here!"

"Hey, buddy." They clasped hands and did a series of motions that ended with them gently bumping their knuckles together.

"You remembered." Jimmy's joy was evident.

"Of course I did."

"And you brought cake? Lemon cake?"

"I was out. I mean the bakery was out of lemon cake, so I got orange. Is that okay? I almost went with the spice, but, well, you know."

Jimmy nodded enthusiastically. "Orange is fine. I mean, it's cake."

"And I . . . had them put white glaze instead of orange. Less color, huh?"

Jimmy smiled. "I'm experimenting," he said proudly. "I ate red gummy bears!"

"You did?" Jack's congratulatory tone was not exaggerated. He knew firsthand about Jimmy's food issues. When Jimmy had been arrested for his mother's murder, he'd had an episode when they tried to serve him spaghetti. Red foods were completely taboo as far as Jimmy was concerned. He truly only liked foods that were beige and tan. Like bread and graham crackers. Chicken nuggets and fries. But Kappy and Edie had been encouraging him to not let that rule his stomach. He was missing a whole world of food out there.

"*Jah.* Kappy said that all food is the same color when you close your eyes. And it's true because color comes from light and there's no light when you close your eyes."

Jack shot Kappy an admiring look, but it was mixed with a smirk. "Is that right?"

"*Jah.*" Jimmy nodded. "And you want to know something? Red gummy bears are good."

Jack chuckled. "Yes, they are." He sat the cake container on the table and turned back to Kappy. "Where's Edie?"

"Right here." She pushed through the door between the kitchen and the dining area as if she had been waiting to make a grand entrance. There was a smear of flour on her nose. "Hello, Jack."

For all her talk about not liking Jack, the words came out on a flirty breath. Kappy may not have had many suitors. Okay, one. But she knew flirting when she saw it.

"You got it wrong." Jimmy looked very disappointed in his sister. "It's 'Hi, Jack.'" He grinned as if he had made the best joke ever.

Jack smiled and turned to Edie. "That never gets old."

"Liar."

He chuckled. "I brought cake."

"And it's orange and I'm going to eat some."

Edie smiled at her brother. "I'm proud of you."

Kappy stood back and watched the exchange. Jack was good with Jimmy, understanding, patient. Even when Jimmy had had his episode in the jail, Jack had been more concerned than irritated. Though she was certain Jimmy's unique needs had been something of a pain to the workers at the sheriff's office. Thank heavens that was over.

Edie had certainly dressed for the occasion in only the way Edie Peachey could. Kelly-green jeans, a long-sleeved, blousy shirt that was so sheer, Kappy could see straight through to the skintight tank top thingy that she wore underneath. The material was thin but printed with that cheetah design that Edie seemed to prefer. Over all, she supposed the outfit itself wasn't all that bad, but it clashed with her cotton candy hair. The blond had grown out enough now that a thin line of brown roots was visible at her part. And to round it off, she had painted her fingernails a deep red.

"I hope you came hungry." There went that flirting again.

Kappy stopped. If Jack and Edie became a couple, then Edie wouldn't be all wishy-washy about whether she was going to leave Blue Sky or stay for Jimmy. She would stay there for Jimmy *and* Jack.

"Of course." Jack patted his waist. He was neither slim nor fat but somewhere in between as if he liked to eat and had to work hard to keep his appetite from catching up with him.

"Good, because we are going to feast."

Kappy wouldn't call their meal a feast, but it did all look good. They carried the food from the kitchen and laid it all out in the dining room.

"I set the table," Jimmy said proudly.

Jack looked at his work with admiring eyes. "You did a fine job."

"I wanted to get on Edie's computer and look for how to make those swans out of cloth napkins. But she wouldn't let me."

Jack gave an approving nod. With Jimmy's limited computer skills there would be no telling what he might stumble across on the World Wide Web. "Folded into a triangle is still very unique."

Jimmy beamed. "And these ones are paper instead so we don't have to wash them."

"Everything looks delicious," Jack said. He shook out his napkin and placed it in his lap, then everyone bowed their heads and said a silent grace.

And he was right; the food looked wonderful. Kappy didn't make such large meals for herself. She didn't see the need in it. Plus, if she cooked a regular-sized meal, she was tired of the food before the leftovers were all eaten. Instead she made a sandwich or ate cheese and crackers. So a meal like this was a treat. For them all really. Jack was a bachelor and knew firsthand the trials of cooking for one, and Kappy knew for a fact that Edie didn't cook like this every day for her and Jimmy.

"I thought we were having chicken." Disappointment colored Jimmy's expression.

"I got a good deal on these pork chops." Edie cut into hers and forked up the bite. "It's good. See." She ate the piece of chop and chewed with more enthusiasm than necessary.

"Pork chops are good," he agreed, "but I really wanted chicken."

"Well, chicken wasn't on sale. Pork was."

Jimmy cut off a piece of his chop and stabbed it with his fork. He held it up in the air and twirled it this way and that. "What is pork?" Jimmy asked.

"You know, bacon, chops, sausage."

"But what *is* it?"

Kappy shot Edie a look, but neither one spoke quickly enough.

"Pig," Jack said helpfully.

It was as if all the air had been sucked out of the room.

Jimmy's fork clattered to his plate. "Why didn't someone tell me?"

Kappy looked at Edie. Edie looked at Kappy. They both turned and looked at Jack.

"Well," Edie started. "I mean . . ."

"I thought everyone knew that," Jack said, his voice apologetic.

Tears welled in Jimmy's eyes. "I didn't." He tossed down his napkin and pushed up from the table. In a flash he was gone, running out of the room and up the stairs. A moment later they heard his door close heavily behind him.

"Is he going to be okay?" Jack asked. Remorse tainted his features.

"He will be." Edie took a couple more bites, a large gulp of her iced tea, then followed after her brother.

Jack stared at the place where she had been.

Kappy could almost feel the waves of remorse and regret coming off him.

"What kind of Amish kid . . . *man* doesn't know that pork chops come from pigs? I mean . . ."

"I know." Jimmy might have some deficient mental capacities, but he was smart enough to know things. "To answer your question, the kind who doesn't live on a real, working farm."

"I suppose." He dug in his mashed potatoes with his fork.

Jimmy's father, Amos Peachey, had died when Jimmy was little. Ruth had her dog breeding business and leased the land they owned to another farmer. They didn't keep animals like pigs or cows to use for meat. Kappy knew for a fact that Ruth had butchered a chicken from time to time, but Jimmy wasn't nearly as attached to live chickens as he was live pigs. Heaven help them all if someone served him duck.

"You didn't mean any harm."

"No." He shook his head but didn't go back to his meal.

They sat in silence for a moment, neither one moving. Kappy didn't much feel like eating a pork chop after that incident, either.

The minutes dragged on. Or maybe those were the seconds. Finally, they heard Jimmy's door open and two sets of footsteps on the stairs.

"Sorry about that," Edie gushed as she came back into the dining room. "Jimmy and I still have a few things to work out, but he has agreed to come back to the table." *Thanks to your cake,* she mouthed to Jack.

"I've come back," Jimmy grumbled, "but I'm not going to eat the . . . you know."

That was big. Amish children were taught from an early age to clean their plates. If the smaller children who didn't understand left something behind, their mother usually finished it. Food was not to be wasted.

"That's okay." Edie nodded, encouraging him with a tense smile.

"I don't want it on my plate."

"I'll ea— take it." Jack held his plate toward Jimmy.

"I don't want to touch it."

Edie started to protest, but Kappy could see that he was close to a complete meltdown. One that would make his earlier outburst seem like a cakewalk. Before her friend could speak, she speared the chop with her fork and dumped it onto Jack's plate.

She wasn't sure how much better that was, but at least the offending chop was off his plate.

Thank you, she mouthed to Jack.

Jimmy carefully scraped the food that had touched the pork chop to one side of his plate. Old habits died hard, and he would finish his meal. Almost all of it, but nothing that could be considered to have harmed a pig.

"I'm not eating that," he declared, pointing to the small pile he had made on the right side of his plate.

"That's fine." Edie nodded. It was as if Jimmy was trying to get one of them to contradict him.

"I'll eat the rest, but not that."

"Okay." Edie continued to eat, but Kappy could tell she was already calculating how long this would last.

She supposed it was just a matter of time before Jimmy's love of animals changed his life. Kappy would have thought it would be something less drastic than turning vegetarian, but it looked like that was where he was headed.

"So . . ." Edie swung her attention to Jack. "How are things at the sheriff's office?"

He all but choked on his mouthful of pork chop. "Uh . . ." Kappy knew what he was thinking. If he said *good,* did that mean crime was up or down? What exactly was good business in law enforcement?

"Any word on Alma?" Kappy thought she would give him an out. Plus, she wanted to know if there had been any news about the bishop's wife's condition or her attacker.

"She seems to be resting and recovering. But I haven't talked to anyone."

"Because it's not a homicide?" Kappy asked. Goodness! She had been hanging around with Edie too much if she was asking such questions.

"Not yet," Edie muttered.

Jimmy took the opportunity since everyone was talking to push his plate away. He had barely managed to finish the untainted portion of his supper.

"There's no reason to believe that the victim will not recover."

"And that means you won't be on the case," Edie said.

"No," Jack returned. "And neither will you."

Edie had the presence to look affronted. "Of course not. I wouldn't dream of meddling in a police investigation."

Jack eyed her with a hooded expression. "Uh-huh."

"So Alma will get better?" Jimmy asked.

"That's what the doctors are saying." Jack nodded.

Jimmy smiled. "That's good. I like her."

"You like her pie," Edie said with a laugh.

"Everyone likes her pie," Jimmy replied, and they all laughed.

Jack stayed for another hour. They finished their meal without any more incidences and gathered around the coffee table with coffee and cake. Jack's orange cake was just as delicious as the lemon he had brought, and Kappy lamented never learning how to bake such things. Maybe that was a blessing. If she could have delicious cake every day, she'd end up bigger than Bishop Sam. She immediately said a quick prayer of forgiveness for her uncharitable thoughts.

After cake, they had talked for a bit, but despite all of Edie's efforts, she couldn't get any more information out of him. Or perhaps there was no more information to get and she was down to simple pestering of a police officer. Was that a thing? Kappy might have to take a trip to the library to investigate.

But not today. Today was a perfect fall Sunday. A church Sunday for her district. There was something special about church Sundays. Something hushed and quiet as if the entire valley were holding its breath in reverence.

The thought was preposterous — tomorrow's word on her calendar. The valley was not holding anything. Church Sunday was not the same for all the many districts there in the valley, but it still felt special all the same. And church Sundays in the fall . . . her heart soared in the cool morning with dew still glistening on the ground. The scent of wood smoke wafted in the air and the valley smelled like autumn. And it brought to mind the upcoming festival. She shouldn't be thinking about that on a church Sunday, but it was the biggest thing to happen until Thanksgiving. The entire village of Blue Sky turned out for the event. English and Amish alike came together to celebrate, compete, and enjoy the last pretty days before the cold weather set in.

Kappy let Elmer out into the backyard with a treat, a ball, and a bone to keep him occupied while she was gone. More than likely he would spend the time she was gone chasing birds, barking at squirrels, and rooting around in the piles of leaves that gathered at the corners of the fence. "And behave yourself," she called as she raced across the yard. She didn't know why she bothered. Elmer was as mischievous as he was adorable.

She shook her head, locked the door, and gathered her things for church. As per her normal Sunday routine, she picked up

Jimmy and together they drove to whatever house the service was being held in. Today church had been scheduled for the Sam Millers' but due to Alma's attack, it had been moved to the James Troyers'. Kappy thought it a shame. Alma had no doubt been cleaning for months. Now she would be put back in the queue and would have to start the process all over again. The Troyers were the next family on the list and though Bertha was the deacon's wife and had surely been preparing for months, Kappy wondered if she had that frazzled look today because she had been fretting over the state of her baseboards knowing everyone in the district would be at her house. Everyone but Alma and Bishop Sam Miller.

"Did you hear?" Jimmy came rushing up to Kappy just before they all went into the house for the service. In this time when the families were still arriving for church, the men gathered on one side of the yard and the women on the other. Kappy hovered on the edges. The women nodded at her by way of greeting, but no one actually stood next to her and drew her into conversation. There had been a time in her life when the separation had stung, not anymore. They meant no harm, but she was the odd man out. She supposed there was one in every district.

She turned to Jimmy. Maybe two. "Did I hear what?"

"The Millers' house was broken into."

"What?" It took everything she had not to screech the word. Could they not catch a break? How many more hits could they take? The last time she saw Bishop Sam, he had been at the hospital, dark circles under his eyes framing the bags that had settled there.

"*Jah.*" Jimmy nodded, his eyes filled with both excitement and worry. "It's something, right?"

"*Jah,*" Kappy agreed. But what? "Where did you hear this?"

"Jacob Detweiler told Mose Peachey."

Both upstanding men in their district. Jacob was Edie's one-time boyfriend, and Mose a small business owner.

"Did they say what was taken?"

He shook his head. "That's the thing. According to Jacob, the only thing missing was a quilt off the bed in their spare bedroom."

Before Kappy could respond to Jimmy's revelation, the call to church sounded and everyone quietly filed into the barn. Kappy was silent while her mind was in turmoil.

127

Why had someone targeted the Millers again? Or had the quilt been stolen when Alma was attacked and no one had noticed until yesterday? Or this morning. Whenever the break-in had occurred.

Mentally, she shook her head to reset her thoughts, then realized the service was almost over and she hadn't heard one word. She had stood when she was supposed to, sang when she was instructed to, and pulled her face into a mask of quiet contemplation as Merv Hershberger delivered the message. Normally, she loved to hear Merv speak. He was Silas's oldest brother and still younger than the rest of the church leaders, but there was a presence about him that calmed the hearts of those around him. It was the district consensus when he drew his lot that God's will was indeed at work that day.

But even so, Kappy couldn't remember anything that he had said. She had a lot of praying for forgiveness to do this afternoon, but for now, during the after-church meal, she would have to listen closely for any more information as to what really happened at the Millers'.

As soon as everything was cleaned up and put away, Kappy and Jimmy made their escape. As long as she was Jimmy's ride to

128

church, she could leave earlier than most. Jimmy had a lot of animals in his care. The sheer number meant a great deal of time was needed and he was excused as were the dairy farmers. And for that, Kappy was grateful. She might be on the fringes, but that didn't mean she could act any old way. Still, she was thankful for the excuse to hurry home from church and share with Edie everything that she had learned.

"What?" Edie's mouth dropped open.

"I said the Millers' house was broken into and the only thing missing was the quilt off the bed in their spare bedroom."

She shook her head. "I don't understand."

"Well, it seems that the quilt was special, something of a family heirloom."

"You should have led with that," Edie grumbled.

Kappy shook her head. "Whoever stole the quilt ransacked the house."

"Ransacked?" Edie asked.

"It's a word."

"I know it is, but how do you —" She broke off. "Oh, right, your calendar." Edie seemed to think about it for a moment. "So the place was torn up and nothing was taken except for the quilt?"

"That's what they are saying."

"But what does this mean?" Edie asked.

"It means I need pigs." Jimmy picked that moment to join them on the porch.

"Give it a break." Edie sighed.

"It means that someone broke into their house," Kappy said. She thoughtfully chewed on her lower lip.

"But are the two related?" Edie mused.

"They have to be," Kappy returned.

"No, they don't."

As much as she hated to admit it, Edie was right: The two incidences didn't have to be related. But why risk going to jail by breaking in the house and stealing a decades-old quilt? Amish quilts were indeed special, but not that special. At least not in Kappy's eyes. What was so remarkable about this quilt?

"Nothing was taken except the quilt," she murmured in a thoughtful tone. "And there's no connection between the quilt and the pie contest. Is there?"

CHAPTER 7

"Listen to this." Edie shook out the newspaper and folded it open. "Pie Vice Judges for Blue Sky."

"Huh?" Kappy wasn't sure what that meant. At all.

It was Monday morning and they were enjoying a cup of coffee while sitting at Kappy's table. Normally, Kappy liked to sit and drink a cup while reading the paper. But as of yet she hadn't touched the daily news. At least she had coffee.

Another day had passed without Alma Miller being brought out of her coma. Kappy was beginning to worry that she wouldn't wake up at all, and they would never know who had attacked her.

"Just listen." Edie cleared her throat and went back to reading out loud. " 'Mrs. O'Malley's Pies might be the best in the country, and today the *Blue Sky News* confirmed that O'Malley's vice president of advertising and sales is in our lovely village. Bobbie Jean Hawkins is reported to have been in town for the last few days and will remain here until after the pie-baking competition that is an honored tradition and sweet part of our fall festival. *Blue Sky News* has been informed that Hawkins has family in the area and is staying with them to keep a low profile until the judging begins.

" 'I don't know about you, but Mrs. O'Malley's Pies are some of my favorites. But I can say without a doubt the Irish baker does not hold a candle to our own Alma Miller when it comes to boysenberry double crust.' "

Like O'Malley's had a boysenberry pie in their lineup.

" 'Other sources tell us that the entrants in the competition will indeed be baking the same kind of pie as all their competitors. This is the first year for this change and the whole village is excited to see how it will (pie) pan out.' "

She folded down one corner so Kappy could see her roll her eyes. Then she flipped it back up and continued to read. " 'This year's flavor? None other than the beloved boysenberry! What are the chances that the winning pie from the last seven years will be baked again and this time by all the

132

entrants? Alma Miller is a shoo-in for the win if she is well enough to bake. We are praying for you, Mrs. Miller, and wishing you a speedy recovery. See you at the festival!' "

"So it is true," Kappy said with a nod.

Edie folded the paper back to rights. Well, she tried to, but corners were sticking out here and there even as she struggled to get everything back in line.

"Here." Kappy took the paper from her.

"It's all true," Edie said. "Bobbie Jean is judge, she works for O'Malley's, and boysenberry is the pie for the contest."

"Changes are inevitable."

Edie shook her head. "I know you're right, but I wonder how Frannie Lehman feels about it all."

"I'm sure she feels the same as with anything else," Kappy said.

Edie snorted.

"What?"

"I bet Frannie is fit to be tied. All these years trying to beat Alma and now having to beat her and her award-winning recipe with the same flavor pie."

Kappy thought about it a moment. "You think Alma will be ready for the festival?"

"I would think. Besides who wants to be the one to let her sleep through it?"

They nodded together, slowly. Alma was one of the most generous and sweetest people that Kappy had ever met. But pie was serious to her. Very serious. Very important. Some women prided themselves on their sewing, their knitting, even the speed at which they completed their laundry. For Alma Miller, this pride was in her pies. And justifiably so. She would not handle being excluded this year, medical issues or no.

Edie was the first one to break their companionable silence. "All I gotta say is, someone better wake her up."

"I've got an idea."

Of course you do. But Kappy didn't say the words. Instead she stood aside and let Edie into the house. They had spent the morning together, first at Kappy's, then they walked up to Edie's to help Jimmy. Once all Jimmy's chores were complete, Kappy had cited that she had work to do and all but dragged Edie home with her in order to escape.

Well, it was possible that she was being a bit dramatic, but it seemed that she and Edie were spending so much time together that she wasn't getting any of her own work done. It wasn't that she didn't like spending time with Edie, she just needed a little time

134

all her own.

She'd had approximately three hours before Edie knocked on her door. At least she got one *kapp* finished and another one almost done.

"Where's Elmer?" Edie asked.

Kappy hooked a thumb over her shoulder. "Out back. What's your idea?"

"Let's go down to the festival grounds and see if we can find out any more about the pie-baking contest."

Kappy shook her head. "How will going down there help?"

"It's not long until the festival opens. I'm sure people are beginning to set up. You don't just have a festival like that in one day. It takes weeks."

Kappy shot her a look.

"Okay, days. But if they are already setting up and I bet you they are, then we might be able to pick up some valuable gossip."

"Or unreliable rumors."

Edie shrugged one shoulder and her top slipped off to expose a strap of pink underneath. At least this time it wasn't shocking pink, but more of a muted bubble gum color. It was almost . . . pretty. Almost girly.

That's when Kappy took a good hard look at Edie. The top she had on was a soft cream color. There was nothing on the front. No kitty cats, no Chinese symbols, no slashing marks of metallic foil claw tracks. And the jeans she was wearing were . . . *blue.* They had holes in them and looked like they should go in the trash, but heaven help her, they were almost normal. For an Englisher that was.

"What are you wearing?" She tried to keep the shock from her voice but was unsuccessful.

Edie looked down at herself. "Clothes?" She raised a quirky brow to go with her smart aleck response.

Kappy flicked one hand up and down, trying to find the words to express all the thoughts zipping through her mind. "Where are the cartoon animals and the animal prints, the too-bright colors and the sparkly stones?"

If she wasn't mistaken, she thought she saw a blush of pink rise into Edie's cheeks. "I thought I might try a little something different."

Kappy looked her friend up and down. "That's different, all right." Edie looked almost normal. Almost. Her shirt still wouldn't stay in place and her jeans looked like they had been run through the meat grinder at the Super Saver, but she was closer.

"Any particular reason?" Kappy asked.

Edie gave another of her negligent shrugs "No." And in that moment, Kappy knew she was lying. But why?

Because she was trying to impress someone and she didn't want Kappy to know. But who?

"Are we going or not?" Edie asked.

Kappy shifted from one foot to the other. "You know if we go poking around, Jack will have a fit."

"Jack's not even on this case."

"Someone is."

"Yeah, and who are people going to be more relaxed around? Two women who are trying to see what the festival is all about or a cop who comes in flashing his badge and taking notes?"

"It could be a lady cop."

"Okay, then, her badge. Who?" she asked again.

"Two women, I guess."

"Then let's go. Jimmy is already waiting in the car."

She should have expected as much but once again she let Edie get the jump on her. Now she was walking around a field at the edge of town watching . . . not much. There were only a couple of trucks and trailers on the property. A shed had been set up on the far side of the lot and a spray-painted sign declared it to be the festival office. It looked a little more like one of the temporary housing units they used after a natural disaster.

"I was expecting more than this." The disappointment was evident in Edie's voice. "Where are the people?"

"There's still two weeks until the festival," Kappy reminded her.

"I know, but I expected . . . more."

Kappy knew what she meant. There was hardly anybody on site, but she supposed next week was when all the pre-excitement would happen.

"A lot of these people travel around and do nothing else but attend these types of events," Kappy said.

"And?" Edie prompted.

"And they are probably at a different festival this weekend, and they'll be here the Monday before our festival."

"I suppose you're right," Edie grumbled.

"Hey!" Jimmy called, jumping up and down. "Hey, Hiram! Over here."

"Hiram?" Edie cupped one hand over her eyes to shade them. "Hiram Lapp?"

"You know any other Hirams?" Kappy

asked with a stilted chuckle.

"Yeah," Edie said. "Three, as a matter of fact."

By this time Hiram had spotted Jimmy and was on his way over. It wasn't like he could miss Jimmy. The young man was jumping up and down and waving his arms in the air like he had just won a million dollars.

Great, she said to herself. Just what she needed. She had about convinced Hiram that the two of them could never be a couple. That any deeper relationship between them would only lead to heartbreak, and now she didn't seem to be able to go through even a day without seeing him.

"Hi, Edie, Jimmy . . . Kappy." Was it her imagination or had he hesitated before he said her name?

"What brings you out here?" Edie asked.

Hiram picked that particular moment to shun Edie. Or maybe he was just ignoring her. Kappy knew Hiram didn't like her running around all over the place with Edie. And that might have mattered to her if they were still a couple. But as it stood now, she was free to do whatever she wanted — given that it fit within the *Ordnung*. He turned away and centered his attention on Kappy.

"I never imagined I would run into you

here." He smiled.

Kappy nodded, feeling something like one of those life-sized mechanical animals she had seen in the kiddie pizza place once. Stiff, unnatural, but still trying to be lovable and accepted. "I think I could say the same thing," she returned.

"I came out to see about getting a booth for the festival."

"Do you still have time to rent one?" Kappy asked.

"I have until tomorrow at three to decide."

"You're going to open a booth?" Jimmy beamed.

"I'm thinking about it."

"I'm going to enter Judith into the small animal category. She's the prettiest rabbit I have. Or hare. Whatever you might like to call them. It means the same thing you know. Well, mostly. Kind of, anyway."

"I'm thinking about entering my own hair." Edie rolled her eyes at Hiram and flipped her pastel-pink-and-blue hair back.

Jimmy laughed. "Not that kind of hair."

"I think it's the best kind of hair," Edie retorted.

"Judith's not really a hare," he said. "She's a rabbit. At first I thought I would enter Judith Junior, but I think he's too young to handle the pressure."

"What kind of booth?" Kappy asked. She felt she needed to say something to keep the conversation going. Or she was going to have to say her goodbye to Hiram and leave. Jimmy and Edie had drifted into their own conversation about rabbits and hare, hair dye, and what the judges would say if Jimmy showed up with a pink-and-blue rabbit for the competition.

"A booth with emergency products," Hiram replied.

"That's a great idea," Kappy said, though she had no idea what he meant. She wanted to support him and if he felt like it was a good idea, then it most probably was.

Like his good idea that the two of you should get married.

Kappy pushed the thought to the back of her mind and willed it to stay there.

"What do you mean, emergency products?" Edie asked.

Hiram didn't even look in her direction.

Edie nudged Jimmy and gestured for him to ask. Kappy was sort of glad; she wanted to know what they were as well.

"What are emergency products?" Jimmy asked.

For a moment Kappy thought he might not answer. However, shunning was one thing and bad manners another. Hiram

Lapp could not be accused of using bad manners, even with the likes of Edie Peachey. "Over-the-counter pain relievers, lip balm, wet wipes, that sort of thing."

"What about bubble gum?" Jimmy asked. "Bubble gum would be good."

Hiram nodded. "I suppose gum should go on my product idea list. If I decide to go ahead with the booth."

Jimmy nodded. "And real bubble gum," he added. "Not the chewing gum kind. You can't blow bubbles with chewing gum. The name even says so."

Hiram smiled and Kappy could tell that he had missed talking with Jimmy. She supposed Hiram didn't see Jimmy as much since Ruth had died and Edie had moved back to Blue Sky.

She would miss Jimmy, too, if she were to, say, marry a black-topper like Hiram and have to change churches.

Not that there was anything wrong with black-toppers. But being a yellow-topper herself, she was from a sect of the Amish church that was a little more conservative than the black-toppers. It wasn't a free lifestyle that worried her. There wasn't that much difference between the groups, but everything would change. She wouldn't be across the street from Jimmy and Edie, she couldn't have a beautiful bright yellow buggy, that shouldn't matter, but it brought her such joy each and every time she looked at it. They were special, those yellow buggies. And . . .

Well, there were a lot of things that worried her, and not least of all were Hiram's continued feelings for his late wife. One day maybe he would be over that love, but until that time, Kappy was living her life. If she was available, then she might give him a chance, but if not . . . well, who knew what living her life might actually bring her.

"It was good to see you again today, Kappy."

"You, too." She smiled as he turned and walked back toward the property entrance where all the cars and buggies were parked.

"Uh-uh-uh," Edie said with a shake of her head.

"What?"

" 'Good to see you again today, Kappy?' When did you see him last time?"

Kappy's temperature rose and she could feel the heat that was no doubt making her cheeks a bright pink. "He may have come by the house the other day."

"And you're just now telling me about this?"

"He just wanted to see what I thought

about Alma."

Edie slammed her hands on her hips and gave Kappy that stare, the one she hated so much. "Tell the truth."

"I am telling the truth." Sort of.

Edie's gaze raked over her as if she were seeing right into Kappy's very being. She shivered.

"The other day, huh?" Edie asked.

Kappy nodded slowly, somehow feeling a bit trapped.

"It was Hiram who told you about Bobbie Jean Hawkins."

"I . . . uh . . ."

"You might as well admit it." She crossed her arms and gave her a self-satisfied smirk.

"*Jah,* okay, fine. Hiram was the one who told me about Bobbie Jean Hawkins."

"I knew it." She slammed one fist into the palm of the other. Kappy didn't bother to point out to her that she couldn't have known anything if she hadn't started getting suspicious about them today. Just a few minutes ago.

"Is there a reconciliation in the air? Please say no."

"Why do you hate him so much?"

"Let me count the ways," Edie said with an over-the-top dramatic flair.

"Count them?"

Edie shook her head. "Never mind."

"Seriously. Why do you hate Hiram so much?"

"I hate everything his family stands for."

"You mean like godliness, hard work, and faith."

Edie flipped one hand in the air as if to dismiss those words. "Not that. The bad ones."

"The bad ones?" Though she didn't ask what *ones* referred to.

"They think they're better than us."

"That wouldn't be very Christian of them."

"True." She stopped as if gathering her thoughts to restart her attack on Hiram's character and family. "Listen, I know what it's like to be afraid of always being alone, but you deserve better than the likes of Hiram Lapp."

The words washed over Kappy like soft, gentle water. There were so many pieces that needed to be discussed, so many that she wished she could hear them all again. "Hiram's not a bad guy," Kappy murmured, unsure of what else she could say.

"I suppose."

Then before either one of them could speak again, Jimmy came up, breathless from running and a red stain riding high on his cheeks.

"EdieEdieEdie." Her name in thrice was one long gush of air. "Edie, you have to come talk to this man. He's a very important man." Before she could respond, he grabbed her hand and physically dragged her toward the animal cages. While they had been talking, Jimmy had been over visiting with a man who was shoveling hay into the various stalls where the horses were soon to be kept. And not just the ones belonging to the Amish buggies, but the ones who would star in the shows.

Jimmy dropped her hand when they got to the man. He was perhaps the biggest person Kappy had ever seen — tall and broad. "Edie, Kappy, this is Tiny."

Edie looked to Kappy and all she could do was stare back.

"Nice to meet you." His voice was gentle, his eyes kindly. But Kappy knew, one squeeze of his hand and he could crush rocks.

"Tiny has pigs!" Jimmy bounced on his toes. "Tell her."

"I have pigs," Tiny dutifully said.

"That is really nice," Edie said.

"What sort of pigs?" Kappy asked. She could tell by the look on Edie's face that she would rather be discussing anything other than pigs.

"I don't have them myself."

Now Kappy was really confused. "Then who does?" she asked as Edie shifted from one foot to another and tugged on her purse strap.

"He knows a man who knows a guy who might have some pigs."

"Jimmy, I just don't think we have room for pigs." Once again Edie started her dig in. How long would she be able to hold out?

"But we should get his phone number," Jimmy instructed. "So when we do have room, we can find him easily."

Edie sighed. "It doesn't really work like that."

"Just get the number," Kappy whispered for Edie's ears. "Then we can get out of here."

"What's your number, Tiny?" She pulled her cell phone from the outside pocket of her purse and proceeded to make a new contact listing for the man who knew how to get pigs.

"Nice to meet you all," Tiny said, giving them a small wave.

Kappy wondered how disappointed he would be when Edie never called.

They said their own farewells, then started back across the field.

"Look." Edie elbowed her before they even got to the parking area. "You see her? You know who she is?"

Kappy turned in the direction she thought Edie was referring to.

"Not there. There." She jerked her head back toward the trailer the festival officials were using as an on-location office.

A petite woman was standing on the small stairs positioned under the door. She didn't look familiar, but Kappy was presented with the back of her. Her hair hung down her back in a low ponytail that was stuck through the back of a baseball cap. It was blond, mostly, streaked through with black and raspberry pink. Her clothing was of the normal Englisher variety: faded jeans, pink T-shirt, and athletic shoes. The jangly bracelets that lined both wrists sort of threw the whole look into something a little less normal, but only made it funky when paired with her multicolored hair.

"Who is it?" Kappy asked.

"Are you serious?" Edie's voice started off near the screech level, then dropped to an almost-whisper. "That's Diana Chamberland."

CHAPTER 8

"That's Diana Chamberland?" Kappy tried her best not to let her mouth hang open, but the young woman was about as far from baker looking as she had ever seen.

Kappy supposed she shouldn't stereotype people, but Diana Chamberland looked more like a Southern beauty queen who had fallen into the masses than a woman who spent most of her time elbow deep in flour.

"I love her hair," Edie was saying.

Her hair was cute, in that crazy, English sort of way. It was the T-shirt blazoned with the name of the bakery, all those bracelets, her manicured hands — were those man-made fingernails? — the makeup, and the perfect tan despite the fact it was already October . . . all those things didn't say baker. In fact, none of them said Blue Sky, either.

"What's wrong?" Edie asked, when Kappy didn't respond.

"I thought she would be . . . older." After all, Blue Sky Baked Goods had been in the same place for decades.

"Oh, right. Well, word on the street is she's the second Diana Chamberland to run the place."

"Huh?" Kappy peeled her attention off the sassy young woman and centered it onto her friend. "How does that work?"

"I heard that Diana Number One got married for the first time at age eighty-two. She retired to Florida somewhere and sold the bakery to the new Diana."

"Really?" Kappy's eyebrows shot upward. "Eighty-two." Maybe there was hope for her after all.

And how strange that the women had the same name and were part of the same family. The Amish did it all the time, but the English? Not so much.

"I heard the new Diana is planning on keeping most things the same but updating a few others." Jimmy picked at a loose thread from his cuff. "Same thing with the recipes."

Kappy and Edie turned in unison to stare at him.

"Where did you hear all this?" Edie asked.

Jimmy shrugged. "People at the bait shop talk."

"The bait shop?"

"Men like baked goods, too. Plus, it's closer to the shop than Frannie's."

"So when you and Mose want a cinnamon bun, you go to Blue Sky Baked Goods?"

"Mel, actually, but *jah*. He goes down to the bake shop, and I watch the bait shop." He grinned in pride.

"That's good," Edie murmured, then turned away as Diana Chamberland disappeared into the trailer.

Kappy knew what her friend was thinking. They could head over and talk to the woman and see if they could gain any more insight into the changes in the pie competition and perhaps how that could have affected the competitors.

"And I heard that Diana One moved down to Florida because she said she couldn't handle anymore cold Pennsylvania winters," Jimmy continued.

"You really shouldn't be listening to gossip," Edie chastised gently.

"People talk," he said simply. "It's not like I can turn off my ears."

Kappy laughed.

"I suppose not," Edie said with a half smile, half frown quivering at her lips. "Now let's go home before we run into anybody else."

Those words must have jinxed them. Before they got to Edie's car, Silas Hershberger and his aunt Maddie started toward them.

Well, not really toward them on purpose, but they were standing right in front of the entrance to the field. The rest had been roped off in preparation for the upcoming festival.

"Kappy, Edie. What brings you here? Hello, Jimmy." Silas's bright smile was as perfect as always and Kappy's heart almost skipped a beat. Or maybe that was from seeing Maddie Hershberger once again. The woman was as sour-faced as ever, as if she had had one too many samples of her not-even-close to famous green church pickles. Everyone in Blue Sky knew that church pickles should be white — at least they needed to be where they lived — but Maddie was determined to convert the entire Amish church pickle eating population of the valley into believers in the green pickle. Kappy wished the woman well, but she knew the conversion would never happen.

"Hi, Silas. I entered my rabbit into the small animal contest. Did you enter anything?" Jimmy asked, the words nearly one long rush of air.

Silas chuckled. "Not myself, but my

mamm has a booth to sell her birdhouses and my aunt is looking into one to sell her pickles."

"It was good to see you." Maddie nodded to each one of them in turn, then faced Silas once more. "I'll only be a little bit," she said and headed toward the office/trailer.

"My sister bought one of your *mamm*'s birdhouses," Jimmy informed him.

"*Jah,* I know." Silas had been there when they had gone snooping around a few months ago looking for clues as to why someone would run Sally June Esh off the road, killing her just as her life was beginning. Instead they had ended up talking to Silas and buying birdhouses.

That was the same day Edie had told her that Hiram didn't like dogs. Why did she remember that now?

"Green pickles?" Edie asked.

"Of course," Silas replied.

Kappy nodded. "She is determined, *jah*?"

"You got to give her that."

"Did either one of them enter the pie-baking contest?" Kappy asked. She wanted to know what everyone else thought about the change of rules. She was certain Alma was happy, Frannie was livid, and everyone else was somewhere in between.

"*Mamm*'s got more than she can do as it

is, and Maddie said there was no way she was going up against Alma Miller's pies. Of course that was before . . ." He trailed off, but he didn't have to finish. That was before Alma had been placed in a coma to try to save her life.

"Have you heard anything about Diana Chamberland?"

"Only that she retired and moved down to Florida. Someone said she was already thinking about opening a bakery down there."

"Not the first one. The one who's running things now."

Silas gave an exaggerated nod. "Oh," he said. "You mean Diana Chamber*land.*"

Chamberland? Chamberlain? Were they really that different? And the answer was yes, of course they were.

"How can they be related if their names are different?" Jimmy asked. Then he frowned. "That didn't come out the way I meant it."

"It's okay," Silas said in that understanding way of his. "I know what you mean, and the answer is they aren't related."

"They aren't related," Edie murmured as they drove home. "How can they not be related?"

154

"Pretty simply, come to think of it," Kappy replied. Though the whole situation had her wondering, too. What had brought the young Diana Chamberland to Blue Sky?

"Maybe she has other family here," Edie continued.

"It's possible, I suppose."

"She moved out here to be with her family and ended up buying the bakery instead."

It was all completely feasible, but something about the theory didn't ring true. She just couldn't put her finger on it.

"She doesn't have any family here at all," Jimmy said from the back seat. He stared out the window, watching the world zip past as he thought about . . . pigs most likely.

"What did you say?" Edie glanced at her brother in the rearview mirror, her voice dropping low with surprise.

"Please watch the front," Kappy pleaded.

Edie switched her attention, but Jimmy continued to stare out the window next to him.

"The Diana woman. She doesn't have family here. She just wanted a change, and this is where she decided it would be."

"In Blue Sky?" Edie asked.

"Who told you this?" Kappy asked.

Jimmy turned his attention around to the two of them. "She did."

■ ■ ■ ■

"I can't believe the things he hears at the bait shop." Kappy sat in the rocker at Edie's and thought about the crazy day they'd had. First Hiram, then Silas, and last but not least, Diana Chamberland. *It boggles the mind.*

They had returned to Edie's to think about what had happened and allow Jimmy some time to work on his presentation with Judith. Kappy wasn't sure what all that would entail, but Jimmy seemed eager to get home. Kappy figured it was nothing more than excitement over the competition that caused him to want to spend even more time with his prized rabbit.

Edie propped her feet up onto the coffee table in front of her and leaned her head back to stare at the ceiling. "I guess it's like a beauty shop, but for men."

"I don't understand," Kappy replied after a moment. She had tried to figure out what the two things had in common but could see none at all. Probably because she had never been in a beauty shop in her life.

She continued to stare at the ceiling. "English women go to the beauty shop and gossip about anybody and everything. In this case, the men are going into the bait shop and telling tales."

"Women, too," Kappy pointed out. "He said Diana Chamberland herself came in."

"It's that honey," Edie said with total conviction. "It's drawing them in like flies to . . . well, honey."

Kappy believed she might just be right about that. Mose Peachey had the best honey in the area, no doubt about that.

"You don't suppose she was trying to get Mose to supply her honey for the contest." Edie's words came out slow at first, then with greater speed as the idea came to fruition.

Fruition. It hadn't been on her calendar that she could recall, and honestly, she had no idea where she had picked it up. At any rate it was a word Kappy cherished.

"Honey in a boysenberry pie?" And Mose's honey at that. She wasn't sure that was a good idea at all. Of course she had never been much of a baker other than cookies and bread.

Then again, neither had Edie.

"If she can put on her card that she used local honey — Mose's honey — then she will have a step up with the judges." She lifted her head and swung her attention to Kappy. Her excitement was palpable. (Now *that* one had been on her calendar.)

"Only the local ones. Bobbie Jean whoever isn't going to know Mose's honey from store-bought corn syrup."

"She might have heard."

"Maybe."

"Plus, there are usually more local judges than out-of-towners."

"True, but what does any of this have to do with Alma's attack?"

"You're right." Edie returned her to original position as if it and it alone was helping her think. "So basically, these facts are just nothing more than a few details to a really interesting, but not helpful day."

After such a busy Monday, the rest of the week seemed to drag by. Alma was still in the hospital, still in a coma, though Kappy had to wonder if she was worse than the doctors were telling them.

Maybe she and Edie were seeing clues where there were none. Lord knew, Edie was good at that. She herself had been known to go a little overboard when it came to figuring out a mystery.

But the fact remained that Alma just might have been attacked at random. The words in the flour a mistake and not really a clue. And all the changes to the pie-baking competition, yet another sign that life moved on. Things change.

Which didn't explain the missing quilt. Or the fact that Alma did indeed write words, clear enough to be read, despite her atrocious penmanship. Or whatever it was called when a person wrote with their finger. And it surely didn't explain the sudden interest in the pie-baking contest.

Kappy took a sip of her coffee and looked at the picture on the front page. She supposed it was a good day if the top story was about the number of entrants in the pie-baking competition in the upcoming fall festival. But according to the *Blue Sky News,* this year they'd had a record turnout. So many that they were talking about a two-round contest. The members of the council that monitored and decided such things were meeting on Monday to determine if that might be necessary. Kappy thought maybe it was a good idea, but she wondered where all the boysenberries were going to come from. She had heard that already, the fruit was getting hard to find in the valley. So many people had entered and were now trying to perfect their recipe or tweak a recipe from a long-dead relative.

A car horn sounded outside. Kappy rose from the table and let Elmer out back. "Be a good doggie, and maybe I'll bring you a new toy from town."

He didn't acknowledge her words, just romped into the backyard, chasing a butterfly who had seemed to have lost his way. Most of them had learned by now to avoid her yard at all costs.

Then Kappy grabbed her purse and locked the front door behind her.

"You really should get a phone," Edie grumbled as Kappy got into the front seat.

"Hey, Jimmy."

"Hey," he mumbled. He had his nose buried in a small hardback book, *Your Bunny and You: An Owner's Guide.*

"He's taking this contest seriously," Kappy commented.

"Which is exactly why I didn't want him to enter." Edie turned the car around and headed for the main road.

"He'll be fine. Stop being an airplane parent."

Edie burst out laughing.

"I got it wrong, didn't I?"

Her friend nodded. "Yep. It's helicopter parent, and I am not being one."

Kappy shot her a look, then folded her hands in her lap. "You most certainly are. You worry about him way too much."

Edie's eyes clouded over, and her entire

demeanor seemed to turn gray. "I can't let anything happen to him."

Kappy turned to see if Jimmy had overheard, but he was still completely engrossed in his reading. "Things are going to happen to him," she said. "And you need to let them."

"How can I do that?"

She shot her friend a sad little smile. "You just have to pray the things that happen are all good."

Edie was silent the rest of the trip to the bait shop. When they pulled up, Kappy could tell that she wanted to go in and snoop around, or maybe just instruct Jimmy to keep listening and report back if anyone said anything about the pie competition. In the end, she did neither.

"Maybe we can get an ice cream when we pick you up this afternoon."

He shrugged. "I'm not a baby." Maybe he had been listening after all.

"I know." Edie smiled, but Kappy could tell his words stung a bit. "But everybody loves ice cream."

"*Jah.* Okay," he said with a nod. He turned to go into the bait shop, then stopped, a thoughtful look on his face. "Ice cream is made from milk, and milk comes from cows. Does it hurt the cows to take their milk?"

Edie shook her head. "Not that I am aware."

"Fine, then," he said. "We can go get an ice cream after work."

He made his way into the shop as Kappy and Edie watched.

"Is he still . . . ?"

"Yes." The exasperation was clear in her voice. "He hasn't touched one bite of meat since our dinner with Jack."

"Heavens," Kappy exclaimed. It wasn't like Jimmy didn't have enough food issues as it was.

"I'm hoping he'll forget about it soon. That it's just the shock of discovery that has him all wiggy."

"Wiggy?" Not on her calendar.

"Freaked out."

Now that one she understood.

"Could be," she murmured. "Any luck getting him to eat tomatoes?"

She held up her thumb and forefinger about an inch apart. "I'm this close."

"Good." Because without chicken nuggets in his diet, Jimmy might just starve.

"Where are we going?" Kappy knew better than to ask. Edie had a mind of her own, and she enjoyed dragging Kappy along behind.

"I'm in the mood for a bear claw."

Kappy shook her head. "I hope you mean the real thing."

"Of course not. I'm thinking since we're so close, let's go to Blue Sky Baked Goods and see what's shaking. That means —"

"I know what it means, and I don't think we should meddle. The doctors are saying they'll take Alma off the medications this weekend and she should be up and around in plenty of time for the competition."

"Who told you that?"

Kappy shrugged. "People talk."

"Mary Raber talks you mean."

"Actually, it was Bertha Troyer and seeing as how she's the deacon's wife, I think that she would know." The last time Kappy and Edie had gone to the hospital, the deacon had been sitting with the bishop, praying and talking, just being with Bishop Sam in his time of need.

"And once she's awake, she'll be able to identify her attacker."

"Maybe."

"Nine babies. ME blue," Edie muttered. "What does it mean?" She paused. "Do you think blue has anything to do with Blue Sky?"

"Why wouldn't she just put the initials, BS?"

Edie shot her a look, then pulled her car into the parking lot at Blue Sky Baked Goods. "Really?"

"Oh." Kappy let out a small laugh. "I guess not."

"Blue could mean a lot of things. Maybe it's how blue connects to ME that we should be worried about."

"I think someone should be worried about the nine babies."

"And I'm wondering how good that bear claw is going to taste." Edie flashed her a grin and got out of the car.

The last time Kappy had been to Blue Sky Baked Goods . . . well, she couldn't remember it had been so long. But she didn't remember the place looking like it did now. The building itself was a standalone shop that had once been a gas station. The pumps were still in the front, though now they had been turned into art. Sort of. They were the kind that were wider on the top than the bottom and had been painted to look like cupcakes. Brightly colored cupcakes with pink frosting, sprinkles, and a chocolate swirl that had once been a hose. It was clever if nothing else and Kappy wondered if they drew in the random passersby or if it

164

was simply because the new Diana hadn't wanted to take the time to remove them as had the old Diana. Diana the First had left them as they were, expecting the visitors to park around them and essentially pretend they weren't there.

Kappy noticed a mother and son standing next to one of the pumps, actual cupcakes raised in salute as a man, most likely the husband and father, took their picture.

"It's something of a landmark," Kappy mused. She didn't get out this way much and hadn't seen the changes. It was tacky and incredible all at the same time.

"Kitsch has become sort of a new thing. I heard there was a giant whale out in Oklahoma. It's pretty interesting, too."

"A whale?" Kappy asked, not bothering to ask what *kitsch* meant. If the cupcake gas pumps were any indication, she could figure that one out on her own.

"Not a real whale. I think it was part of some swimming pool area. When the pool closed, they left the whale. People go inside and everything."

"Seriously?"

"You can look it up."

"And people go there and what?"

Edie shrugged. "What they do anywhere else I suppose. Buy T-shirts and postcards, take pictures for Facebook and Instagram."

Kappy knew Facebook, but Instagram was a new one on her. "And then other people want to come visit and it brings in more money when they buy T-shirts —"

"And cupcakes," Edie supplied.

"And pies." Kappy nodded to the customer just leaving the shop, two bright pink pie boxes stacked one on top of the other.

Pink seemed to be the theme. The building itself was pink on pink, the window trim painted a couple of shades darker for contrast. But all that pink made the blue of Blue Sky stand out even more. Maybe Diana Chamberland wanted her own chance to put Blue Sky on the map.

"Come on." Edie headed for the door, Kappy close behind.

The inside of the bakery smelled pretty much like the inside of any other bakery: yeast, sugar, and vanilla. In a word, heaven. Several workers milled around behind the counter, putting cookies, bear claws, and cronuts into little pink sacks. Cupcakes were stored in little pink boxes, and pies in square flat ones. Cookies by the dozen had their own shape of pink box as did the donuts. All the workers wore pink T-shirts like the one they had seen Diana Chamberland wear at the festival office. All wore pink baseball hats and jeans. And smiles. Big smiles, as if their job was the best one in the world. Kappy could think of plenty of jobs worse than serving up sweets.

But something about it seemed a little fake. Maybe the word was forced. As if Diana ruled with a pink iron fist and everyone had to be happy, or else.

"What exactly are we looking for?" Kappy asked. She wouldn't mind looking at a cupcake or two.

"Anything suspicious."

"I think all this kitsch is suspicious."

"What?"

"I think Diana is trying to make Blue Sky a tourist destination. Like that place you were talking about in Ohio."

"Oklahoma."

"*Jah.* Oklahoma. If she can get people to come here and see her cool bakery, take pictures with her unique art work, and buy her yummy products . . ."

"She would make a mint."

"And if she wins the pie-baking competition, she would get a lot of attention statewide."

"And from there, she would take over the world."

"Huh?" Kappy gave Edie a blank look.

"It's just an expression. She wants to

reach her goals and one person is standing in her way."

"Alma Miller."

They both looked over to the bakery owner.

"She doesn't look like the kind who could commit murder," Edie said.

"Alma's not dead."

"Don't you think that was the original plan? Go in, hit her on the head, steal her recipe, and run?" Edie asked.

"She could do that without killing her."

"I thought you said she didn't look like the kind who could whomp somebody in the head."

"No," Kappy said patiently. "You said that."

"But you agreed with me."

Kappy shook her head at Edie's twisted logic, but it was true. Diana Chamberland didn't look like that kind of person. But desperation could have people do all sorts of crazy things. If not desperation, then urgency to succeed. True, the bakery appeared to be very successful, but that didn't mean it was at the level Diana wanted to reach. Especially not if she were trying to build a tourist attraction there in Blue Sky.

"Can I help you?"

Edie jumped at the question. And Kappy's heart pounded as if they had just been caught sneaking in the back.

They had been standing there so long thinking about almost-murders and giant cupcakes, that everyone in front of them had been served.

"Yes, uhm . . . What is the flavor of the day? You do have a flavor of the day, right?" Edie sounded as if she was ready to pick a fight if there wasn't one.

The smiling girl in the pink T-shirt and matching ball cap moved to one side so Edie could get a better look at the chalkboard behind her. It stood out since it was black against the pale pink walls, but the chalk was of course, pink.

"As you can see, the flavor of the day is chocolate with sea salt caramel drizzle and whipped buttercream frosting. We offer it in gluten free, sugar free, gluten free/sugar free combo, non-peanut/non-tree nut versions, as well as vegetarian and vegan." And there was the smile again.

"Does it just come regular?" Edie asked.

The smile wavered a bit. "Uh . . . of course." She looked flustered that they didn't have any special requests. Kappy supposed that was just the way the world was turning. Jimmy wasn't the only one who had special food needs.

She opened the display counter in front of her and pulled out a scrumptious-looking cupcake. It was the size of a toy truck, beautifully decorated with an angular piece of chocolate planted in the center of the creamy frosting. Kappy was certain there were enough calories in one bite to last her all week.

"Make that two, please," Edie told the girl. "And two coffees."

"Edie," Kappy whispered. "We promised to get ice cream with Jimmy." That would be way too many sweets for one afternoon. She would end up with the sugar shakes.

"So we take him a vegetarian cupcake. He'll be happy."

"Can you add a vegetarian cupcake, too, please. And make that one to go."

"Of course." The girl looked almost re-lieved. "Vegetarian or vegan?"

"They're not the same?" Edie asked. Kappy was just as lost in such matters.

"Oh, no, vegans don't use any animal products. They avoid butter, cream, leather shoes."

"Heavens to Betsy, please do not tell my brother about leather shoes."

The girl drew back. "O-okay. I'll do my best."

Edie smiled. "I didn't mean literally. Sorry."

The girl waited, tongs in hand, expectant look on her face.

"Oh," Edie started. "Vegetarian is fine."

"For now," Kappy teased.

"Don't even say it," Edie said as they sat down at one of the sturdy pink tables scattered around. None of them appeared to be the same and not one looked to be new. The chairs were just as mismatched except for the pink. It was as if Diana had bought everything at an auction and painted it one afternoon. Kappy figured that was about the truth. Only the deep blue tile floor offered any relief to the pink.

"So what do you think?" Edie asked.

But Kappy didn't have time to answer.

"Fancy finding you two here."

Edie dropped her plastic fork — pink plastic fork, no less — and smiled. "Jack Jones, on the case or not?"

"Or not," he said, holding his tie in place as he sat down at their table.

"Sure, grab a seat," Edie said. "We'd be glad to have you join us."

"Maybe if I sit here long enough, I can find out what the two of you are really up to."

"We came to get a cupcake." Edie pointed

171

to hers with the prong end of her fork.

"I don't believe that's the reason for even one second."

"All right," Edie said. "We've been found out, Kappy." She turned her full attention to Jack. "We came here to see if this is where you've been getting those delicious cakes."

For a split second the self-assured cop looked almost guilty, then he recovered quickly. So quickly that Kappy wondered if she had even witnessed the change at all.

"And that is my little secret." He smiled, but his eyes seemed reserved. "Nice outfit," he said to Edie.

She looked down at herself as if just now noticing what she was wearing. "Thanks."

Kappy blinked. What was going on here?

For the second day in a row, Edie was dressed almost plain. Well, by Edie standards anyway. Today she wore a soft yellow shirt that complimented the pastel colors in her hair. Her jeans were dark blue, but soft looking, worn-in somehow. Slip-on canvas shoes covered her feet. She might have been a soccer mom or a grade school teacher. She definitely didn't look like the Edie Kappy had first seen all those months ago.

"Thanks," Edie said again. "But it's nothing."

Jack's smile deepened. "Well, you look nice."

That's when it hit her. Edie had changed the way she dressed in order to impress Jack! Kappy wasn't sure whether to be proud of her for taking that step or shaking her for changing for another person.

Was it a change for the good or would it end up breaking her heart?

One thing was certain, she needed to talk to her friend about it and soon. But just not right now.

"So I heard that you were the one who monitored the drawing to choose the pie flavor for this year," Edie said. "How does it feel to take part in such an historic event?"

Jack stretched out his long legs and chuckled. "I'm not sure I would call it historic."

"Believe you me," Edie said. "This is one for the books."

Kappy kicked her under the table.

"Ouch." She smiled back at Jack even as she bent to rub her shin. "What I mean to say is with all the extra excitement between the change in the rules and Alma being attacked . . ." She stopped. "This is a festival I'm sure we're not likely to forget anytime soon."

"Any leads on who attacked Alma?" Kappy asked.

He smiled that not-telling-you-anything smile and picked at the end of a straw wrapper. It must have been left on the table by the previous customer. "There are always leads."

She didn't believe that for a second. But she smiled in return as if he had completely answered her question.

"I just can't believe that would happen to the poor bishop's wife," Edie said. Her voice held more than a touch of the dramatic.

Jack's dark gaze met Kappy's. "Seriously?"

"Can it, sister," Kappy said out of the corner of her mouth.

Jack laughed, and that was completely her intent. Get him to relax. He wouldn't tell them anything if he thought they wanted to know.

"How's Jimmy?" he asked.

Edie held up the pink box. "Vegetarian cupcake."

Jack winced. "Sorry about that."

"It was bound to happen sooner or later."

"I had no idea."

Who would? Everyone, it seemed, believed that all Amish kids knew everything about farm life and farming, and animals and a host of other things that weren't correct. Most all that Jimmy knew about animals dealt with mating, birth, and loving, feeding, and caring for them. He had never once thought about animals as food. His life wasn't centered on that.

"It's okay, really."

"So no meat at all, huh?"

"None." Edie shook her head.

"I guess the next time I come to supper I should bring some Not Dogs? You know, tofu hot dogs."

Edie thought about it a second. "Are they red?"

"Pink," he said.

"I'd hold off on that a while. We're not quite there yet."

CHAPTER 9

"Next time he comes to supper . . ." Kappy said as they drove back to get Jimmy.

"Stop."

"Don't think I don't see what's going on here."

"And what's that?"

"He's talking about coming to eat with us again and bringing food. You're dressing like . . . like . . . well, like a regular old English woman." Kappy stopped, shaking her head. "I don't know what to make of it all."

"There's nothing to make of anything." Edie patted her hair.

"You like him."

"It's no secret that I like Jack. Everybody likes Jack."

"But you really like Jack. Like-like Jack."

"Maybe. But . . ."

"But what?"

"But he doesn't seem to notice me."

"Not the truth."

"Criticizing what I'm wearing or telling me to butt out of his investigation is not what I mean."

"He wouldn't criticize what you wear if he wasn't noticing."

"Negative attention is better than no attention at all? Is that what you're saying?"

"I guess so." Kappy turned a little in her seat so she could better see her friend. "It's like the little boy in school who first pulled your hair. Or messed with the back of your apron."

"Or put gum in my seat?"

"Who put gum in your seat?" Kappy asked.

"Jacob Detweiler."

"Really? I had no idea."

"Yup. Third grade. And it got all over my best green dress. Oh, I remember that dress. It was the perfect color of lime green, not too bright, not too pale —"

Kappy snapped her fingers under Edie's chin. "Focus."

"Right."

"At the time it made you angry, but now you know that he was just trying to tell you that he liked you."

"I get that. But Jack Jones is a long way from eight years old."

Kappy shot her a look. "I don't have to be in a relationship to tell you that any man isn't far from eight years old, not when love is involved."

Edie winced. "Ouch," she said.

"Am I wrong?"

"No. Sadly enough, you are right on the money."

Jimmy was over the moon with his vegetarian cupcake. "Can I eat it in the car?"

"Sure," Edie said the word, though she didn't seem quite as confident as she spoke. That was another thing. She had been keeping her car really clean. Making an effort, that's what Aunt Hettie always called it. Edie hadn't known they would be running into Jack today, yet she had dressed differently just in case. Making an effort. "Just hold over the box so you don't get crumbs all over."

He nodded and untied the little string separating him from sugar bliss.

He grew quiet as he ate. He was two bites in when he asked, "What makes this different than a regular cupcake?"

After the conversation they'd had with the smiling girl at Blue Sky Baked Goods, Kappy had no idea. It wasn't like it was chock-full of steak or bacon. It could have eggs, butter, and milk unlike the vegan cupcake.

They turned to look at each other, realizing at the same time they'd paid double for a regular ol' cupcake all due to a very clever marketing plan.

Saturday the buzz was all about Bobbie Jean Hawkins and the big pie-baking competition. Kappy normally stayed clear of her basement, allowing her customers to come and go as they pleased, and somehow she still managed to pick up on the excitement. Everyone was talking about it, and if all the people entered who said they had, it seemed that half the residents of Blue Sky were registered.

Kappy had to wonder if it had anything to do with the fact that Alma was still in her coma. The doctors were assuring everyone that come Monday they would wean her off the medications and have her back on her feet in a couple of days. She felt they were being overly optimistic but with modern medicine, she supposed anything could happen.

But the *big* buzz was the rumor that the winner of the pie competition would have their recipe chosen to be a part of the Mrs. O'Malley's line. The women were talking about traveling to the home office wherever it was and meeting with the CEO of the company, flying on private jets (surely the bishop would overlook it one time for such an honor), and having their face put on every pie box sold. Why else would a big executive like Bobbie Jean Hawkins come and judge their small local contest? She had to be getting something out of the deal and that something was a new pie recipe.

Kappy believed none of it. But the excitement was a bit infectious.

Sometime after lunch she put Elmer on his leash and started to Edie's. It was too beautiful of a day to sit cooped up in the house and both of them could use a bit of fresh air. Though she'd had to buy Elmer a new harness. This one didn't allow him to pull her along. She needed it because he spent half their walks choking himself and the other half trying to jerk her arm out of its socket. This was better for both of them.

Jimmy was out front when she and Elmer caught sight of him. He waved in that enthusiastic way that only Jimmy had.

"Where's your sister?" Kappy called.

"She's inside." Jimmy grinned. "And boy is she going to be glad to see you."

"Why? What's going on?"

Just then, Edie flew out of the house as if

the devil himself was on her heels.

"Kappy, thank goodness you're here. We've got to get down to the festival grounds right away. I just heard that Bobbie Jean Hawkins is having a press conference."

"A press conference for pie." Kappy shook her head.

"It's about more than pie," Edie countered.

"I like pie," Jimmy said from the back seat, but he was too busy petting Elmer to show much more enthusiasm than a quiet statement.

After Edie had made her announcement, she had hustled them into her car and together the three of them — four with Elmer — drove to the festival grounds.

"It's a pretty big deal around here," Edie pointed out.

"Maybe, but it's still just pie."

Apparently, Kappy was about the only one in Blue Sky who felt that way. English and Amish alike had turned out for Bobbie Jean Hawkins's press conference.

"Let's see if we can get up closer to the front," Edie said. That might prove impossible, seeing as how the conference was just about to start and they were among the last to arrive.

They started across the parking area toward the trailer where the media people had set up to record the show, or maybe put it on television live — she didn't know how to tell the difference. But the closer they got to all the ruckus, milling people, and crew members testing the equipment, the more antsy Elmer got. He danced sideways on the end of his leash as if by turning his body he could somehow lose the harness and run free.

Then he dropped to his rear, raised his nose into the air, and howled. He wasn't used to crowds or so many strangers all at the same time. He could handle a few here and there, like her customers arriving and going down the back stairs into her basement. This was way too much for him.

"I told you we should have dropped him off at the house," Kappy reminded Edie.

"If we had, we would have been late." As it was now, they were just in time.

"Jimmy, would you mind taking him back to the car?"

"I'll take good care of him."

Edie cast a worried glance at Jimmy. "Do you remember where we parked?"

"Jah."

"And you think you can find it on your own?"

He frowned. "Of course."

"I can walk with you if you like." Kappy knew that cost Edie a lot. She wanted to get close to the stage so she didn't miss a word of whatever it was Bobbie Jean Hawkins had to say.

"You're helicoptering again."

"Is that even a word?" Edie asked, clearly trying to ignore his accusation.

"It's never been on one of my calendars." Kappy gave a shrug.

"It means, I got this." Jimmy tugged on Elmer's leash, somehow getting him on his feet, and turned around. "I'll be in the car with Elmer if anybody needs me."

"Don't talk to any strangers," Edie called as he walked away.

"I know, Edie." He said the words but didn't turn around.

Kappy thought she might call out some other reminders as he walked away, but she managed to hold her tongue and simply watch him.

"He'll be fine," Kappy said.

"I know." But she still sounded worried.

"Come on." Kappy linked arms with her friend. "Let's go see what we can find out about this pie business."

Between the number of women and men crowded around and the excitement that hummed in the air, it felt a little like the festival had already begun.

"Is this on?" Deb McDonald, mayor of Blue Sky, tapped the microphone, sending a dull thumping sound followed by a screech racing through the speakers. "Whoa." She chuckled. "Sorry about that. I'd like to thank everyone for coming out today. Saturdays are important to us all, and I'm glad you spent part of yours with me. Many of you may have heard about the changes in the pie-baking competition this year, I can only believe that these changes will make us stronger as a community.

"I'm not going to go through them one by one. If you didn't get a list of them before when you registered, be sure to pick one up now. There are plenty, and everyone can have a copy.

"Now on to the real reason why we're here. Folks, we've been trying to get a big judge here for our pie-baking competition for a long time now, and I'm proud to say that this year we have been successful. Ladies and gentlemen, I bring you the vice president of accounting and sales for Mrs. O'Malley's Pies, Bobbie Jean Hawkins."

The crowd exploded into applause. A few whistles rang out as the mayor stepped aside, still clapping, and Bobbie Jean took her place.

She was a short woman with a bright smile and a cap of shiny brown curls. As any good baker should be, she was on the round side, though Kappy got the feeling that she had to constantly monitor what she ate in order to keep her weight at a manageable level. Her eyes were a sparkling bright blue and a sense of familiarity stole over Kappy. There was just something about her.

"Thank you. It's a thrill to be here today. I know a lot of you have questions about the changes to the judging, entries, and even the type of pie everyone will be baking. I'm here to answer any of those questions that I can. The rest will have to be fielded by your madame mayor."

Laughter rang out. Bobbie Jean waited for the noise to die down before continuing. "I'd like to begin with the questions the media has prepared."

"The media being old man Johnston with a pencil and a notepad," Edie muttered.

"Shhh," Kappy said.

"Ms. Hawkins, we are so very glad you're here. And please don't take my question the wrong way. But why here? Why Blue Sky?"

"I've heard a few rumors around that I have a relative in the area, and that is absolutely false. I feel your festival has the

185

down-home feel that Mrs. O'Malley's Pies is famous for. What better place to serve the community?"

"So you're not here to find a new pie recipe?"

"Goodness, no." She seemed overly surprised by the idea, as if she had never heard of such a thing before.

"She heard the rumor about a relative, but not about the search for a new pie recipe?" Edie whispered.

"She didn't say that," Kappy whispered back.

"She didn't have to."

"Shhh," the person in front of them shushed as Edie's voice had gotten a bit louder. "Do you mind?"

"Sorry," Edie whispered, quieter this time.

"I stumbled upon Blue Sky in a marketing survey and came to take a look," Bobbie Jean was saying.

Kappy figured she had been asked the question about choosing Blue Sky over any of the thousands of small towns across America. Any of them with a fall festival, a state fair, or a county fair would have been more than happy to host an almost-celebrity and have her judge the pie-baking contest. She supposed it was a little like having Elvis Presley judge a singing competition. If he weren't dead and all.

"I'm just thrilled to be able to share this experience with you."

"She sounds like she's runner-up for the Miss America pageant."

"I don't even know what that means," Kappy replied.

The woman in front of them glared over one shoulder but turned back around without a fuss.

Edie stuck out her tongue once she was facing front again.

"I suppose if the rumors of looking for a new pie recipe aren't true, there are going to be a lot of disappointed bakers out there."

Bobbie Jean smiled. "Remember, I just said that it wasn't the main reason I came to Blue Sky, but who knows? If something strikes me as a recipe Mrs. O'Malley's can use, well, anything is possible."

Anything is possible.

Those words spread hope through the Blue Sky baking community quicker than water can fall through a crack.

"What sort of name is Bobbie, anyway?" Kappy asked as she and Edie sat at her kitchen table trying to decipher the last words Alma had written before she lost consciousness. "For a girl, I mean."

"Short for Roberta, I guess." Edie shrugged and took a quick sip of her spiced tea. It was a sure sign that fall was on the way. "Why?"

"I don't know. It suits her, wouldn't you say?"

Edie shrugged again and set her mug on the coaster. "I guess. I mean, I suppose it does."

"She's just so spunky and full of life," Kappy said. Once again that sense of knowing her or having known her eased over Kappy. It was a bit unnerving. "Does she look familiar to you?"

"I don't know. Maybe a little, I guess. Why?"

"She seems . . . like someone we know."

"They call that déjà vu. Sort of."

"What's it mean?" Another word not on her calendar.

"It's French." She shook her head. "I'm not sure how it really translates, but it's a feeling that you've been somewhere before or some of the same things are happening to you that already have. Like you're living a part of your life over again."

Kappy shook her head. "This is different. I feel like I know her from somewhere."

"Maybe she looks like someone you know,

188

and you are getting the two of them mixed up."

"We know all the same people. Who does she look like to you?"

"No one." Edie's answer was entirely unhelpful. "Like Bobbie Jean Hawkins."

"You are not making this any easier," Kappy said.

"Why is this bothering you so much?"

"I don't know. But I feel it's important. Is that part of déjà vu?"

"Not that I know of. Déjà vu is more of just a feeling. It comes and goes."

And this had been staying with her for a while. Or maybe she was just worried over nothing. Still, she couldn't help but feel there was some connection she wasn't making.

They were still pondering the hows and the whys of déjà vu a couple of hours later when a knock sounded at the door. Jimmy had just come in the back from completing his chores. He was determined now more than ever to do them all on his own to prove to Edie he could handle the responsibility. It wasn't that the chores themselves couldn't be handled by one person, but his faithfulness to do the work was supposed to make her see reason in letting him add to his

189

menagerie. (That meant *zoo*. It had been on her calendar a few months back, but she couldn't remember exactly when.)

"Hang on," Jimmy called, his hands under the water as he washed up in the kitchen sink. That was Edie's rule: Rinse off outside. Soap and hot water once you were inside.

"I'll get it." Edie pushed up from the table and made her way toward the front door.

"It'll just take another second," Jimmy said, his voice turning a bit urgent over . . . answering the door?

Kappy turned in her seat, peering out the door that led to the living room to where Edie was just now reaching for the doorknob.

The knock sounded again.

Edie opened the door. She gasped.

Jimmy groaned.

"Uh, hi," Jack said. He was the only one who had spoken so far and yet he knew something was up.

"Jack, what a surprise." Edie pushed her glasses onto the top of her head as if she shouldn't wear them all the time and stood back to allow him to enter. "What brings you out this way?"

"You invited me to have supper."

"I did?"

Kappy bit back a laugh. She knew where

this was going.

"I thought you did. I mean . . . Jimmy." They both said his name at the same time. But he had already let himself out back.

"Jimmy called me and said you wanted me to come to supper. So I came to supper."

"And you brought cake," Edie said, with a quick glance at the plastic container he held in one hand.

"I can go."

"Not a chance." Kappy eased around and relieved him of the cake. "Come on in." She set the container on the table. "I'll go get Jimmy."

Once the cat was out of the bag and he knew the gig was up, he had headed out the back door.

"Is she mad?" he asked as Kappy came down the back steps.

"A little stunned."

"But not mad?"

Kappy shook her head and sat on the middle step, her feet on the one below. "Want to tell me what this is all about?"

Jimmy shrugged and kicked at a clump of grass. "I don't know. I just want her to be happy."

"And inviting Jack to supper without telling her is going to make her happy?"

He shot her a sheepish grin. "When you put it that way, I guess not. But I can tell she likes him."

"Of course she likes him."

"I mean likes him-likes him."

Kappy shrugged. "Maybe."

Jimmy shot her a look. "I might not be as smart as other people, but I've got eyes."

Kappy laughed. "Okay. I think you're right."

He beamed. "That's better."

"But I think it might be better from now on not to surprise her like this, okay?"

He nodded as she stood.

"And Jimmy," she said as they prepared to go back into the house. "You're one of the smartest people I know."

The moment be walked back inside, Jimmy apologized to his sister and Jack. They both told him it was okay, of course, and Edie set herself to figuring out something for them to eat for supper.

"And please don't cook any animals," Jimmy asked as Edie started for the kitchen.

"None at all?" Edie asked. Her tone was serious, but her eyes twinkled as she waited for his response.

"None." His answer was emphatic.

"What about for us?"

He thought about that a moment. "I would rather you didn't, but I can't dictate what you eat and what you don't. Only myself."

"Dictate?" Edie asked, one brow raised in question. "Where'd you learn a word like that?"

"Kappy taught it to me. It was on her calendar."

"Oh, the calendar." Edie nodded sagely.

"What's this?" Jack asked.

"Kappy's got this calendar that has tear-off pages with a word on it for each day."

"The challenge is to use the word the day it comes up on the calendar, but if nothing else it gives a person the chance to improve their vocabulary."

"That's interesting." Jack tilted his head to one side. "And the bishop doesn't care about this?"

Kappy shook her head. "What is it with you English? The bishop doesn't have his hand in every little thing that his congregation is doing."

"So he doesn't care if you have the calendar?"

She wasn't one hundred percent positive of that. But she was eighty. Okay, maybe seventy-five. But that was still up there.

"What about your Sherlock Holmes novels?"

"What about them?" Her back stiffened despite her resolve not to let this conversation get to her.

"What does he think about the mystery novels you hide under your bed in that old box?"

"I might not have ever gotten around to asking him about them."

"Convenient."

Kappy threw a dishtowel at Edie, who laughed and ducked into the kitchen.

"Seriously, though, the bishop, well, one of them for the white-toppers —"

Kappy held up one hand. "Let me stop you right there. The white-toppers are so much more conservative than us yellow-toppers or the black-toppers."

Big Valley was home to three different types of Amish: the Reno, the Nebraska, and the Byler.

The Nebraska Amish, or white-toppers as they were known in the area, were among the most conservative types of Amish in the country. The Bylers, or the yellow-toppers, were in the middle and that's what Kappy and Jimmy were, yellow-toppers. The Reno, or black-toppers, were the least conservative of the Amish in the area, but Kappy had heard that the Lancaster County Amish, who were also Old Order, were much more progressive than the black-toppers from Kish Valley.

"And there's really that much difference?"

Kappy understood. To the outsider the differences between the yellow-toppers and the black-toppers appeared to be the color of their buggies. The white-toppers dressed a bit differently, wearing brown pants instead of black, and kept to themselves.

"That's like comparing a honey crisp to granny smiths. Both are great, but they are two different things."

"Even though they're both apples?"

"Right."

Jimmy scratched his head. "I'm confused."

Jack patted him on the shoulder. "It happens to the best of us."

Supper was a happy affair as usual. Edie recovered quickly from her surprise at finding Jack on her doorstep and ready to eat. Somehow she managed to piece together a meal that suited everyone. Jimmy had been studying on what was meat and what wasn't, something he had never thought much about before. Kappy was certain it wouldn't be long before no one could trick him about such matters.

After they ate, they settled into the living room with cups of coffee and the delicious looking cake that Jack had brought.

"What's wrong?" Edie asked as they enjoyed their dessert. Well, everyone but Kappy seemed to be enjoying it. Instead of eating she had been pushing the same bite around on her plate.

"You don't like chocolate?" Jack asked.

"It's not that."

"I thought all women liked chocolate." Jack's tone was close to sad betrayal.

"It's delicious." Kappy took a bite to prove it. The cake was good. More than good, but other things running around her mind were keeping her from enjoying it. "Today, when we were listening to Bobbie Jean Hawkins, she seemed familiar. I can't seem to shake that déjà vu or whatever."

Edie chuckled. "You don't shake déjà vu. You learn to live with it or you let it go."

"Then maybe this is something more," Kappy mused. She took another bite of the cake just to balance everything out. "What's more than déjà vu?"

"A hunch," Edie said.

"A what?" Kappy asked.

"Not on your calendar?" Edie asked.

"A hunch is when you just know something in your gut," Jack supplied.

"That's what I have, then," Kappy said. "I feel in my gut that I've seen Bobbie Jean Hawkins before."

CHAPTER 10

"Maybe she's famous," Edie mused. "You know. Like on one of the television commercials for Mrs. O'Malley's Pies."

"Jah," Kappy said. "Because I watch so much television."

Jack chuckled.

"Maybe other advertising, then," Edie said with a sniff. "Like magazines. I know you read those when you go to the doctor."

"I don't think I've ever seen an ad in a magazine for pies, but if I have, what would the vice-president be doing as the spokesperson?" She might not know much about how the English world worked, but she did understand that jobs like that were reserved for models and actors.

"Maybe she just looks like somebody you know," Jack offered.

"Maybe," she murmured. That could be it. Bobbie Jean Hawkins definitely seemed familiar, though Kappy could never remember meeting her. "Where is she from?"

Edie used her phone to tap the Internet. "Says her family is originally from Pennsylvania but she lives in Ohio now. That's where the home offices for Mrs. O'Malley's Pies are."

"I wonder where in Pennsylvania," Kappy mused.

"It doesn't say."

"What's she doing judging such a small contest?" Jack asked.

"That's what I want to know." Edie nodded like the importance of the answer ranked right up there with who shot President Kennedy.

"There's been all sorts of rumors why, but no one knows for certain."

"Rumors?" Jack asked.

"You haven't heard?" Edie exclaimed. "They've been making their way through the baking community. Oh, wait. Of course you wouldn't have heard. It's not like you bake and have anything at stake here."

Jack cleared his throat. "No. Of course not. So what are these rumors?"

"That whoever wins the pie-baking contest will have their recipe picked up by Mrs. O'Malley's Pies."

"Really?" Jack's brows raised in interest. "Any truth in this?"

"That's what everyone's been wondering. I think there is," Edie added. "After all, why would a big executive be at a small country festival if not to try to score a box of recipes."

"Wouldn't it have been better if the contest remained the same. You know like when they all baked different pies? They would have more . . . recipes . . . to choose from. That's it." Jack smacked one fist into the palm of his other hand.

"What's it?" Kappy's heart leapt in excitement. Something about the tone of his voice sent tingles through her.

"Alma's recipe box."

"What about it?" Edie asked.

Jack visibly shook himself. "Nothing." He stood. "I've got to go."

"Wait." Edie stood and laid one hand on his arm. "Alma's recipe box is missing from her house?"

Jack stuttered. "Why would you think that?"

"You got all goosed when we started mentioning pie recipes. That's it, huh? Alma's recipes are gone."

"I can't say." He cleared his throat again.

"You don't have to."

Kappy watched the exchange between the two of them.

"If Alma's recipe box is missing that means whoever hurt her got what they were after," Edie said.

"If they were after the pie recipe. Which I still don't believe." Jack shook his head, but Kappy wasn't quite convinced. For the time being she was staying out of it.

"People will do all sorts of crazy things for whatever means a lot to them." Edie shot him a pointed look.

"But pie?" Kappy blurted out. "It's just pie."

"And it's totally possible," Jack agreed. "But I've said too much. I gotta go."

Edie released his arm and allowed him to leave. She didn't say another word, just waited for the door to close behind him, then turned back to Kappy.

"Alma's recipe box is missing."

Kappy nodded. "But that means whoever took it already has Alma's pie recipe."

"If it was Bobbie Jean Hawkins, then she will have to go through all the motions of the festival in order not to be suspected."

"What if it wasn't Bobbie Jean Hawkins?" Kappy mused.

"You mean someone like Frannie Lehman?"

"*Jah,* or even Diana Chamberland. Either

of them could make a fortune with that recipe."

Thoughts of missing recipe boxes, cryptic messages written in flour, and swinging iron skillets plagued Kappy's thoughts and dreams all through the night.

Considering everything that had been taken from Alma's home — a quilt and a recipe box — the attacker had been after something specific. Kappy didn't know much about investigations, but common sense said this was no ordinary break-in. This was no run-of-the-mill attack. And not a random crime. Jack was smart enough to figure that out, but Jack wasn't on the case. Not really. It wasn't like he couldn't gather evidence, but he had his own cases to work. He wouldn't be trying to figure this one out. Kappy had no idea how good or bad the detective on Alma's case was. As much as she hated to admit it, even in her thoughts, as long as Alma was alive she might be stuck with a mediocre investigator who didn't give two wits about the Amish of Blue Sky.

That was one thing about Jack Jones: he cared and respected the Plain people in the valley. He had always been dutiful, never condescending. He seemed to genuinely care about the people he had sworn to protect whether those people drove automobiles or buggies. It was one of the many reasons Kappy liked him.

Just after sunrise she got out of the bed. She let Elmer out, but she could tell that he was still half asleep as he trotted down the porch steps and into the grass. It was early for them both, but lying in bed, her mind twirling like a windmill in a storm wasn't doing any good at all.

It was Sunday and an off Sunday for her district. Getting up and working was out of the question. She would like to sew this morning. Making the stitches, concentrating on each pleat and praying as she made the *kapp* would have soothed her like nothing else.

Instead she curled up on one end of the sofa and retrieved her crochet basket. She pulled out the rainbow-colored scarf she had started and smoothed it across her lap. It was what the English called a stash buster. There were so many colors in the pattern that it almost hurt her eyes. It wasn't a stash buster for her. She worked mainly in black, white, and a couple of pastels for the small girls in the church. Occasionally she would crochet them scarves to wear in the winter. Pink, yellow, and baby blue were okay in her district for the little crowd, though the women all wore black. This piece could not be categorized into either of these. But it was so Edie. Kappy smiled and ran her fingers over the stitches. She supposed she should say that it was so Edie from two weeks ago. Something had happened in the time since Alma had gone into the hospital till now. And she wasn't sure exactly what had caused this change in her friend, but she had an idea. Edie liked Jack Jones. She hadn't come right out and said the words, but she didn't have to. Kappy could tell. She just hoped her friend still liked the colorful scarf come Christmas morning.

Elmer scratched at the back door. Kappy put her crochet away and went to let him in. She would work on her pet project later. For now it was time for the Sunday paper, a cup of coffee, and seeing what news was worth printing today.

She made her way to the front door, Elmer trailing along behind her.

"I really should teach you how to fetch the paper," she mused as she made her way across the front yard to where the Sunday morning paper had been tossed by the English driver who brought it by each week. Elmer ignored her, found a stray toy that had somehow been dropped in the front yard, and proceeded to tear it to little pieces.

Kappy looked down at her newspaper. "Then again, maybe not." She turned back toward the house. "Hup," she called to the dog. "Inside."

Elmer picked up his toy and started behind her, dragging the soggy thing along with him.

"Oh, no you don't." Fall was coming. Dew coated everything, making sparkles all over the yard. It was pretty to look at but messy when it came to bad dogs who wanted to run through the water giving no thought to coming back into the house and tracking mess all over Kappy's clean floor.

Elmer shot her a sad, puppy dog look, but dropped the ripped-up toy and followed her into the house.

Kappy took the towel off the hat rack next to the door and wiped his feet and belly. She also dried the tips of his ears that tended to drag in anything and everything. "There."

She gave Elmer a new toy from the basket she kept by the door and made her way to the kitchen. He followed behind her, new treat in his mouth. Kappy laid the paper on the table while she made her coffee, then sat down to look at the paper. There on the front page was the article about Bobbie Jean

Hawkins and how she had come to town to judge the pie-baking contest. The rumors were addressed, basically just the way they had been explained to them at the press conference. But there were other parts of the article that bothered her. There was a picture of Bobbie Jean and right next to that was a picture of what Kappy assumed was supposed to be Alma's hand. In reality it could have been practically anyone's, but since the Amish who had been baptized didn't allow their picture to be taken, she was sure this was the best this reporter could do given the time frame. At least he was respecting the Amish *Ordnung* on the matter and not violating Alma that way. The poor woman had been through enough now as it was.

The words under her picture were what captured Kappy's attention. All the doctor's plans were laid out there. How the doctors had been keeping Alma in a coma in order to help her heal. How they were planning to take her off her heavy medication on Monday and reassess her condition at that time. They also recounted how Alma was considered the Amish queen of pies in the area and everyone was wondering if she would be well enough to compete in this year's upcoming baking contest. The writer had even speculated as to why Alma had been attacked, hinting that maybe foul play had been involved.

Was she the only one who didn't think pie was worth dying for? Or important enough to kill for? Maybe so.

She folded the paper back to rights, then headed for the kitchen to cook herself some breakfast.

"I wonder if the recipes were taken from the Millers' house when Alma was attacked or during the second break-in." Edie dipped a pretzel into the small bowl of ranch dressing sitting between them.

"You should eat more carrots. Or celery," Kappy said.

Edie made a face.

It was midmorning on Monday and the pair had taken a break from helping Jimmy do a deep cleaning on the dog pens. It was something he did about every six weeks. It kept the fleas and ticks out, removed any scat they might have otherwise missed, and in general was one of the reasons Ruth, and now Jimmy and Edie, had some of the best dogs in the valley.

"How are you going to convince Jimmy to eat more colors if you don't eat them yourself?"

"I just wish he'd eat more meat."

"More?" Kappy asked.

"Any," she corrected. "I wish he'd come in now and eat."

"I know," Kappy said. "But he's not going to starve to death just because he's cleaning the dog pens. If he's hungry enough, he'll come in and eat. You have to trust him."

"It's not him I don't trust." The words were uttered so quietly that Kappy was uncertain at first if she had even heard them at all. She jerked her gaze to Edie's. Her friend's brown eyes were serious and pleading.

"He's fine, Edie. You're not going to break him or ruin him if you let him have a bit of freedom."

"So he can go around painting all the doors in Blue Sky?" She laughed but a couple of tears worked free. She wiped them away with the back of one hand.

"I'm surprised he hasn't painted yours yet."

"Only because he thinks Jack doesn't know what it means." She sighed. "It was so much easier when he was younger."

"Of course it was. If he was in danger, you could just pick him up and move him out of the way. But your mother loved him, and she raised him well. He knows right from wrong. He's read his Bible. And he has God on his side. The rest is just faith."

"Faith," she muttered. She said the word as if it were part of a foreign language.

And Kappy knew. It had been a long time since Edie Peachey'd had faith in anything other than disappointment.

"Faith." Kappy gave an emphatic nod.

Edie picked up another pretzel, dipped in to the ranch, then just held it there.

"You could start going to church again."

Edie drew back, a horrified look on her face. "Amish church?"

"If you want, but I was thinking more of maybe the Lutheran church or one of the others there in town. Of course you can always go back to Delilah Swanson's church."

"Heavens, no." Edie dropped the pretzel and covered her ears as if the words might burn them.

The pair plus Jimmy had met Delilah in the summer when they were helping Jack (without Jack actually knowing it) find the person who ran Sally June Esh off the road, killing her in the process. Delilah was different than any preacher's wife Kappy had ever seen. Short hair, short tops, short . . . shorts. She wore her makeup heavy and perfect and tottered around on too-tall shoes even at

209

the benefit carwash. Edie had called her the perfect combination between Liz Taylor and Marilyn Monroe. The next time after that when Kappy went to the library she looked up the two women on one of the computers there. She had to admit that Edie's description was right on all accounts.

"You could invite Jack to go to church with you."

"Are you kidding?" Edie dropped her hands from her ears as if nothing could block out the horrible ideas spewing from Kappy's mouth.

"No. Not at all."

"I couldn't do that."

"You could."

She shook her head. "No."

"Maybe he already goes to church."

"What does that have to — oh, no."

"If he goes to church already, you can just go with him."

"I am not taking a date to church."

"Why not? The Bible says, 'For where two or three are gathered together in my name, there am I in the midst of them.' "

"So we get Jimmy in here and have church right now."

"Would you be serious?"

"I am serious."

Kappy pressed her lips together in disapproval, then relaxed her mouth the minute she realized she had to be the picture of her aunt Hettie. "Just think about it, please."

Edie picked the pretzel out of the dip and set it aside on her napkin. Then she took a carrot stick from the tray of veggies and dunked it into the ranch. "Maybe."

Kappy smiled. "That's the spirit."

"All done." Jimmy beamed. He had spent a hard morning at work, but he looked energized instead of ready to drop.

For that, Kappy could tell Edie was grateful.

"Can we go get ice cream?" he asked, wiping his forehead with one sleeve.

"Not until after lunch."

"I figured that." Jimmy's tone bordered on disgusted. Or maybe it was just frustration. How was he supposed to learn anything about being an adult, if she hovered over him all the time?

"What does that mean?" A light of challenge lit in Edie's eyes.

"Just that I know you won't let me do anything out of rhythm."

"Rhythm?"

"You know, just how things work."

"I can go out of rhythm," Edie huffed.

"I guess. Sure." He wiped his face again.

"I'm going to take a shower."

"You do that," Edie said. "And when you're finished we're going to town."

Jimmy's mouth fell open like it had a bad hinge on both sides. "To eat lunch?"

"To eat ice cream."

"Whoop!" Jimmy punched the air with his fist and bounded up the stairs.

"Are you serious?" Kappy asked. There was no going back now. If Edie changed her mind, Kappy was sure that Jimmy would have an utter meltdown. And that would not be good.

As if to prove her point, Edie palmed her keys and waited by the door for Jimmy.

"I can't believe we're doing this," Kappy said as they rolled along.

"We're doing it, Ethel." Edie's words were pushed through the side of her mouth.

"Who's Ethel?" Jimmy asked.

"Exactly what I want to know," Kappy said.

"If you guys are going to be like this, then ice cream lunch will not be very much fun."

"Ice cream lunch." Jimmy grinned. "Can we make this a thing? Do it once a week?"

"Once a month," Edie countered.

"Every other week?"

Edie smiled. "Deal."

■ ■ ■ ■

It felt good to get out for no other reason than to slurp down some fantastic ice cream and sit around with her friends. Kappy was sure they presented quite a picture: an Amish woman, an Amish young man with Down syndrome, and a plainly dressed English woman with cotton-candy-colored hair.

Even though Kappy had talked with Edie a bit about not changing for another person, it seemed Edie hadn't been able to accept that advice. And it was getting worse. Today she had on a plain gray T-shirt and a regular pair of dark blue jeans. No holes, no faded marks, just jeans. On her feet she wore canvas slip-on shoes in the unlikely color of white. Not bright white, just a dull, cotton white. And dressed this way, she didn't seem like Edie at all.

This was way past making an effort. This was trying too hard.

And the fact that the chance they would run into Jack Jones was slim to none made her nisus seem even more desperate. *Nisus* was her word for tomorrow — she had peeked. But she was glad she knew it. *Striving toward a certain goal or prize; Impulse.* It fit the situation perfectly. This seemed very impulsive as far as Kappy was concerned. Did Edie like him that much, enough to change?

Or was it that she disliked herself even more?

"You think we might run into Jack?" Kappy asked as they sat at the table in Yoder's Creamery and ate their ice cream.

Yoder's was an independently owned and operated dairy farm that had branched out into ice cream, churning their own cream for their small parlor. The place itself was a tribute to the black-and-white Holsteins, with black-and-white-spotted walls and depictions of the iconic milk cow on every available surface. The ironic thing was the fact the Yoder farm preferred the heavier cream content of the soft brown jersey cows to the milk-producing Holsteins. Kappy supposed that plain brown walls wouldn't have quite the same appeal.

"Why would I think we would run into Jack Jones?" Edie scoffed, but the words seemed as forced as her high-pitched laugh.

"I like Jack," Jimmy said. "Maybe he can come to our next ice cream lunch."

"Better than that," Edie said, shifting in her chair as if gearing up for a rant. "Why would you even say that?"

"I didn't mean any offense."

And it was clear that Edie had taken some. "It's okay." She settled back in her seat, the tension in her body still visible.

"But I'm worried about you." Kappy flicked a hand toward her friend, then took another bite of her ice cream to allow for the pause. "You've been dressing so conservatively. I know why you're doing it. And it's not right."

"I don't know what you mean."

"She means," Jimmy started, "that you're dressing so plain, like a boring English woman instead of weird like you always do and that is weird."

Edie looked from Jimmy to Kappy, who nodded. "It's true."

"What is this, some kind of ice cream intervention? Did you plan this?"

"No." Jimmy's emphatic word was enough to convince Edie. She relaxed back into her chair, well mostly.

"Jimmy, can you get me a napkin and a little cup of extra chopped almonds?" Kappy asked.

He was on his feet in a heartbeat.

"Let me get you some money." Kappy reached for her purse.

"Don't worry about it. I got it." He

bounded off to the counter to wait his turn in line.

"Do you like Jack that much? Enough to change yourself and who you are?"

To Kappy's dismay, tears filled Edie's eyes. "I don't know who I am," she whispered. "I never have. I thought I would find myself in the English world and all I found was that it's hard to be away. But I'm stubborn and I did it anyway."

"But you're back now."

She shook her head. "I know what you're thinking, and I can't rejoin the church. I just can't."

"I've said it before. You should go to another one."

"You really believe God is the answer?"

"Of course He is. Not changing how you dress to attract the attention of a man who already likes you. Just the way you are."

The tears spilled over her lashes and rolled down her cheeks. Edie wiped them away with her fingers before they dripped off her jaw. "You really think so?"

"He'd be crazy not to."

Just then, Jimmy bounded back over with the cup of nuts Kappy had requested.

"Invite him to church," Kappy said. "Then see what happens."

CHAPTER 11

"What happened there?" Jimmy asked, his voice overloud in the small confines of the car.

They had finished up their ice cream and were on their way back home. Jimmy was wired from eating so much sugar, but Edie needed to relax and not try to control everything. If that meant Jimmy would be bouncing off the walls for a couple of hours, so be it.

Kappy turned to look. Four police cars, two fire trucks, and an ambulance were haphazardly parked outside Blue Sky Baked Goods.

"Something big from the looks of it," Edie murmured.

"I would say so." But before Kappy could utter another word, Edie swung the car around and pulled in next to a familiar silver sedan.

"Is that Jack's car?" Jimmy asked.

"I think so," Kappy said, noting Edie's small smile and flush of pink in her cheeks.

"We probably shouldn't be here," Edie said as she put the car into park and turned off the engine.

"Nope," Kappy agreed.

Jimmy stared out the back window, trying to get a better look at all the happenings. "I can't see anything," he reported.

"Should we take a closer look?" Edie asked, but her hand was already on the door handle, set and ready to push down and release the lock.

"I guess we're going to have to," Kappy said. How else were they going to know what happened and if it had anything to do with the pie-baking competition or Alma Miller and her attacker?

Barely controlled chaos. That's how Kappy would describe the scene they encountered in the parking lot of Blue Sky Baked Goods.

People milled around the lined asphalt, talking with police while pointing and gesturing toward the building.

"What happened?" Kappy breathed, resisting the urge to turn in a full circle and take it all in. She had been to two murder scenes and neither one of them had looked like this.

But there was no one around to answer that question and yet people were everywhere. Aunt Hettie would have called this a frenzy.

"I might have known."

Kappy whirled around to find Jack Jones standing behind them. Apparently, her calculations concerning feasibility needed some work.

"Hey, Jack," she said.

Jimmy shook his head at the missed opportunity.

Edie fluffed her hair.

"What are you doing here?" Jack asked.

"I could ask you the same thing. Someone hurt?" It was better than murdered but not as accurate.

"No," he said simply.

"Then I should definitely find out why you're here." When Jack showed up, it was because people were dead.

"I hope you weren't buying donuts." Jimmy slapped his leg and laughed.

But Kappy knew Jack wouldn't tell them what was going on. He may have let it slip that Alma's recipe box had been stolen, but he had been socializing with them. His guard had been down. Right now he was in full-out cop mode and not giving an inch.

But he didn't have to. There were too many first responders in the parking lot barking orders and yelling to be heard over the sheer noise of the cars, the nature that surrounded them, and the ordinary people still hovering around.

"I was getting a cake for Heather. You remember Heather."

Edie nodded. She had known her much better than Kappy, but then again Kappy had been on the fringes of her own community, she surely didn't fit in with the cool, out-crowd who hung out with the English kids.

"She had her baby and today is her first day back at work. She's having a hard time adjusting to being away from him, so we thought we'd buy her a cake to cheer her up."

"Or make her cry harder because she'll never get the baby weight off if she keeps eating sugar," Edie countered.

Jack looked horrified as if he had committed some kind of social felony.

Kappy elbowed Edie in the ribs and not very gently she might add. "I'm sure she'll appreciate that very much." Heather was the type of person who was always doing good for others. When Jimmy had been charged with his mother's murder and put into jail with the rest of Blue Sky's criminals, it was Heather who had given him games, coloring books, crayons, and grape-flavored

220

ice pops that weren't red and therefore tolerable to him. He might have not been comfortable in jail for the two weeks he was there, but Heather had at least made it a bit brighter. Kappy made a mental note to add Heather to her prayer list.

Oh! She should crochet Heather a baby blanket. Kappy had always wanted to do that.

"So she had a boy?" Kappy asked.

Jack nodded but didn't have time to answer as one of the firemen walked by talking on his cell phone. The words *bomb threat* rang out loud and clear.

"There was a bomb threat?" Edie's voice was loud enough to be heard two counties over.

"Shhhh." Jack grabbed her by the elbow and hustled her away from the milling crowd. "Not so loud. Some of these people are fragile and we just got everyone calmed down."

Fragile or strong, Kappy felt like she would be a little freaked out with a bomb threat hanging overhead, so to speak.

"There was a bomb threat?" Kappy lowered her voice so that only the four of them could hear. In the back of her mind she wondered why Edie was being so quiet, but that was Edie, never predictable except in her own unpredictability. Or maybe this was just one more ploy to get Jack to notice her.

"Yes, but as far as we can tell it was a prank."

"Some prank," Edie muttered.

Jimmy was looking from one of them to the other. "Why would someone want to play such a mean joke?"

Edie patted his arm reassuringly. "Some people are just like that, Jim."

"No one was hurt?" Kappy asked.

Jack shook his head and checked his watch. Kappy was a little impressed that he still wore one. Most English men she had seen used their cell phones to tell time. This one small measure made Kappy realize that Jack was a little old school. But that didn't mean that Edie needed to change to suit him. Not if she really liked him, and Kappy had a feeling she did.

"What are you three doing out this afternoon?" Jack asked. He wasn't one for the niceties, so Kappy felt like he was just trying to change the direction of the conversation.

"We took Jimmy out to get ice cream."

"For lunch." He nodded with typical Jimmy enthusiasm.

Jack drew back a bit and turned to Edie. "Wow," he said. "I'm impressed. Or are you just getting soft in your old age?"

"Not funny, Jonesy."

He continued to chuckle while Edie frowned.

A uniformed officer walked up. He nodded toward Kappy, Edie, and Jimmy, then he tugged on Jack's sleeve and whispered something for only him to hear.

Jack's smile disappeared. He drew back. "When?" he asked in a low voice.

"Sometime last night."

Jack nodded. "Thanks for letting me know."

The officer dipped his chin and made his way back to the throng of policemen clustered between two of the cop cars.

"What happened?" Edie asked.

Jack hesitated and Kappy supposed he was deciding whether to tell them. He cleared his throat, his expression hooded yet uncomfortable. "Alma Miller died last night."

"It just doesn't make sense," Kappy said. "Everyone was talking about how good she was doing. And how they thought she might even be recovered enough for the baking competition."

Edie nodded. "I know."

They had returned to Edie's house after Jack had left them in the parking lot of Blue

Sky Baked Goods. Jimmy was beside himself all the way back to the house and had gone outside to sit among his animals to calm down. He found the goats to be particularly soothing, or so he had told Kappy once.

"How? Why?" Kappy asked no one.

"Maybe what we should be asking is who?"

Kappy sat back in her seat. "Oh, no. We're not going there. Who would hurt Alma?"

Alma Miller was one of the sweetest souls Kappy had ever met. She took her role as the bishop's wife very seriously. She always had a smile on her face and a piece of pie for whoever stopped by.

"Pie," Edie said as if she had heard Kappy's thoughts.

"No." It was the only word Kappy could manage.

"It's the only thing that makes sense. Frannie Lehman —"

"We are not blaming Frannie Lehman for a murder we do not even know happened."

"You don't have to be a hotshot detective to see what's going on here."

"Alma took a turn for the worse. It was God's will."

Edie shook her head. "It was the will of someone who wanted her dead and the only reason for that would be her boysenberry

224

pie recipe. And that was, most likely, the same person who conked her on the head."

"You think that Frannie Lehman hates Alma enough to one, hit her with the intention of killing her, then, two, go into the hospital and finish the job? It just doesn't make sense."

"It makes perfect sense. And that's what's so sad about the whole thing. Here's Frannie, who has worked her entire life to build up her bakery. Her recipes are her livelihood and yet she could never beat Alma, who baked because she simply loved it."

"If you know so much, then how did she do it?" Kappy sat back and crossed her arms in a silent challenge.

"Easy. She snuck into the hospital and plugged a syringe full of air into her IV line. That's all it takes."

"In fantasy land maybe. Or Hollywood. In the real world it takes much more air than that to kill someone through an IV line."

Edie's eyes widened. "How do you know?"

Kappy felt her face fill with warmth. "I read, you know."

"You didn't get that from any Sherlock Holmes story."

The heat intensified. "Maybe I've been reading a few other things."

"What? Like Stephen King and Lee Child?"

Kappy sniffed. "Maybe."

"Maybe my butt. I wonder what Bishop Sam would say about you reading that sort of trash."

"It's not trash. They are very talented writers."

"Maybe so, but that still doesn't fall within the *Ordnung.*"

"My reading habits are not the issue here."

Edie shot her a sly grin. "We'll come back to that. So maybe it's not a syringe full of air. Maybe it was poison or lighter fluid. I don't know. It could have been vanilla extract for all I know."

"I don't think you can kill anyone with vanilla extract."

"Not the issue here."

"And what is the issue?" Kappy asked.

"That Frannie Lehman killed Alma Miller to eliminate her competition for the pie-baking contest."

"Why just Alma? What about Diana Chamberland?"

But she had fed Edie just what she wanted. "The bomb threat at Blue Sky Baked Goods. That was intended for her."

"We don't even know if there was a bomb."

"But there was the threat," Edie said.

"Called in," Kappy countered.

"Probably from one of the phone shanties. Or even a pay phone."

"I don't think there are any more pay phones," Kappy pointed out.

"Stay with me," Edie coached.

"It's crazy."

"Not so crazy. You just don't want to believe the lengths that people will go to in order to get what they want."

Kappy sighed. "If it involves killing another for a pie recipe, do you blame me?"

"No," Edie said. "But there is one way we can find out the truth."

"What's that?" Kappy was almost afraid to ask.

"Let's go over to Frannie's Bakery and see if any threat has been made to her."

She shouldn't have agreed to it. But she had. Now here she was again, riding down the road with Edie in the driver's seat and Jimmy in the back. Kappy loved having Jimmy around, but she had kind of hoped that Edie would leave him at home. He knew that Alma Miller had died, but he didn't know she was murdered.

Truth be told, they didn't, either, but Kappy couldn't deny that her death seemed a bit suspicious. All the news they had heard had been positive. The medical coma they had put her in was to allow her to heal. The doctors had stopped those medications and were waiting for her to come around. No one, no one at all, expected her to die.

But when they had told Jimmy they were heading to the bakery, there was no stopping him.

"Can we get some cookies for later?" he asked. They were almost there, and he had been making a verbal list of all the things he wanted to get.

"Don't we still have some of the cake that Jack brought over?"

He let out a light chuckle. "No, I ate the rest of it yesterday."

Edie caught his eye in the rearview mirror. "If you keep eating like that, you're going to get chubby."

"I already am." He patted his stomach with pride.

"All right, then," Edie said. "If you're okay with it, so am I."

Edie pulled her car to the side of the road in front of Frannie's house. Like Edie and Kappy, she lived off the main road with neighbors and fields on both sides of her house. Kappy wondered if perhaps Frannie leased her land to farmers in order to make ends meet. Kappy and Edie both did the same. There was too little farm land left in the valley to allow any to lie fallow for long.

"Or maybe we can find a cake like the one Jack brought over the first time." Jimmy got out of the car and closed the door behind himself.

"Haven't we already been through this?" Edie locked the car and together the three of them made their way onto the path that led around to the basement bakery.

It hit Kappy then that Frannie only did business out of her basement, a policy that Kappy herself followed, but was criticized for enforcing. Not that she really cared. She didn't want people knocking on her door when they could take care of it all themselves if they simply did as she asked.

"Kappy?"

She shook herself out of those thoughts and turned to Jimmy. *"Jah?"* She had a feeling he had called her name a couple of times before he got through.

"What are you going to get?"

"I don't know." They made their way down the stairs and into the dimly lit bakery.

There weren't quite as many people there today as had been the last time they had come. But business still looked pretty good. Rosie M stood at one worktable decorating a birthday cake with delicious-looking lavender flowers and green swirly embellishments. Susie Lehman ran the cash register while Frannie helped customers with their requests.

Frannie looked up, caught sight of them, and several emotions crossed her face, beginning with surprise and ending with something akin to resignation.

Kappy got the distinct feeling that she wasn't happy to see them. And it made her wonder: Had their reputation for digging around when someone died become a thing? They had only helped solve two crimes there in Blue Sky. It wasn't like they were a detective group, or whatever it was called. Agency. That's right. And it wasn't like they *tried.* These things just seemed to come to them. Well, maybe Edie tried a bit, but that was only because she was bored. Kappy knew it.

"What can I get for you?" Frannie asked.

"A dozen cookies," Edie said.

Frannie didn't move.

"Oh, for pity's sake," Edie cried. "Kappy." She grabbed Kappy by the elbow and propelled her forward.

"A dozen cookies please," Kappy requested.

"Chocolate chip," Jimmy supplied even

before Frannie could ask. "No wait. Sugar cookies with icing. No, chocolate chip."

Frannie gave a tight smile, a weird expression for a woman who always frowned. "How about a half dozen each?"

Jimmy's eyes widened. "You'd do that for me?"

There was that tight smile again. "Of course."

"Then, *jah*. Please." Jimmy's grin was as bright as the sun.

Kappy smiled to herself. He really was a jewel.

"I suppose you heard about Alma Miller?" Frannie asked as she handed the bag of cookies over the top of the counter. Jimmy took the bag and stood back to wait for them to finish.

"Jah," Kappy said. "We heard."

"It's a shame," Frannie said. "Can I get you anything else?"

Kappy looked back to Edie.

Her friend waved a dismissive hand. "Whatever you want is fine. I'm sort of over this."

For all her acting like Blue Sky meant nothing to her, Edie was sure hurt when she was shunned according to the *Ordnung.*

"Two of the caramel cupcakes, a half dozen bagels." Those would be good for

231

breakfast next week. "And . . . what are those?"

Kappy pointed to a new display. The cookies were strange, they looked like peanut butter but were shaped like fire hydrants and bones.

"All-natural dog treats."

And she said the words with a straight face.

Kappy blinked. "Seriously?"

"Of course." Tight smile again that seemed to say Frannie was tired of the conversation. Or maybe she thought they were there to question her more about where she was when Alma Miller died.

"Cross my heart." She made the motion, but this time her expression didn't change. Kappy had heard somewhere that it took more muscles to smile than to frown. Maybe her face was simply tired.

"Huh." Kappy eyed the treats. They looked good, like even people might be able to eat them.

"It's just something new we're trying." As far as explanations go, it wasn't the best, but it would have to do.

"Let me have two of them."

"I take it you still got the dog you got from Ruth Peachey after she died?"

"*Jah,* he's still all puppy, but I'm having

232

fun with him."

"You should get him a buddy. Rosie M's litter of cow dogs are about ready to go. I'm sure she could set you up with one."

Kappy pasted on a polite smile. "Thanks, but Elmer keeps me busy enough as it is." *Him and running around with Edith Peachey.* But she didn't say it.

Frannie shrugged as if it was no big deal. "Suit yourself, but if you change your mind . . ."

"I know where to go."

Kappy paid for the items and they made their way out of the bakery shop.

"Why didn't you ask her about Alma?" Edie screeched once they were back in the autumn sunshine.

"You can't see? That woman is innocent."

"That woman is hiding something."

"Maybe, but that doesn't mean she's guilty."

They were almost to the car when Edie turned around and started marching back in the direction they had just come. "I'm going down there again."

"And what?" Kappy asked.

"I'll tell her I forgot bread or something."

"She's not going to talk to you. You're shunned, remember?"

"She'll talk to Jimmy. I'll give him the

money, and he can ask her the questions."

Jimmy stumbled a bit at the thought of talking for his sister. If anything, Edie had spent half her life talking for Jimmy.

"What are you going to have him ask?"

"I dunno. If she was at the hospital last night. What she thinks about Alma. If she knows anything about nine babies, ME, or blue whatevers."

"I'm sure she knows a few things about blue," Jimmy said. "She's almost a grandmother and all."

"Thanks, Jimmy." Edie started back down the steps. Jimmy followed behind her. They let themselves into the bakery once again before Kappy expelled a low growl and headed after them.

Thankfully, when Kappy got back inside, Jimmy and Edie were still standing in line waiting for a turn to talk to Frannie.

"So good of you to join us," Edie said with a self-satisfied grin.

"Let me do the talking," Kappy said even though she had no idea what she was going to say. She only had two customers to think about it before it was their turn again.

"Did you forget something?" Frannie asked.

Kappy cleared her throat. "Will you come talk to us for a few minutes?"

"About?"

"Alma Miller."

"No." The word was clipped.

"Frannie, with all the competition between you and Alma, it's only a matter of time before the police are here. Wouldn't you rather have an opportunity to go over your story before they ask?"

She stopped, braced her hands on her hips, then she exhaled heavily. She untied her apron. "Amanda, I'm going to take a little break. Can you . . . ?" She gestured toward the counter.

Amanda's gaze darted from the three of them to her mother before she nodded. She hadn't been in the bakery a few minutes before. Kappy figured she had been on a break and was now back working.

"Let's go upstairs." Frannie nodded to the set of stairs that led from the basement into her house.

It was hard to tell if she was mad that she'd had to stop work and come talk to them, or if it was just her normal demeanor. Kappy supposed it didn't matter as long as she talked to them.

Frannie led them just into the kitchen and motioned for them to have a seat around the small table there.

"What's this about?" she asked the very

235

second everyone had found a place. No coffee, no niceties.

"I'm concerned about you," Kappy said.

Edie choked, coughed, then managed to recover.

"Why is that?"

"Because I don't think pie is a good enough reason for one person to hurt another, but there are other people involved that aren't as certain as I am."

She stiffened. "Like?"

"The police. Now that Alma is dead . . . I mean, they'll be around to find out what you know."

"They've already come around. And they already know what I know. I don't have any more information than I had when she was first attacked."

"And you don't know what the words in the flour mean?"

Frannie frowned. "What words in the flour? What are you talking about?"

Kappy and Edie exchanged a look.

"Detective Jones didn't show you the message Alma left in the flour?"

"No."

"It said nine babies, ME, and the word blue. Does that mean anything to you?"

Frannie shook her head. "Nothing."

"Do you have a piece of paper where I

can write it down? Maybe that will help." Kappy felt as if she was reaching for nothing, trying anything to make something come of this visit when it was a bust from the start.

Frannie looked like she might protest, then she rose to her feet, pulled open one of the kitchen drawers, then returned to the table with the requested items.

"Like this." Kappy wrote out the words and turned the paper around for Frannie to see better.

Frannie looked them over, then pushed the paper back. "I really need to get back to work. We have a huge order going out tomorrow."

Kappy laid a hand on her arm and stopped her from getting back to her feet.

"If we can't figure this out, you'll be the first one in the suspect line."

Frannie eased back into her seat and pulled the paper close once more. She read the words slowly. Then again.

"Nine babies, that doesn't make much sense at all. ME blue —" She stopped.

"What is it?"

"It didn't make much sense when I read it to myself, but now that I've said it out loud. ME blue could be referring to Alma's sister Amelia. That's what everyone called her: Emmy Blue."

CHAPTER 12

"Are you sure about this?" Edie looked at the house, then back to Kappy.

"It's the only way. She's the one person who will know for certain."

"And you trust her memory?"

"I don't think we have much choice." Not if they wanted to keep their dealings a secret.

After Frannie had dropped her bomb about Alma's sister, she refused to say anything else. Citing that she had to get back to work, she hustled them out of her kitchen and back down the stairs. Before they knew how it happened, they were standing outside Edie's car.

They had decided then to get Jimmy back home and regroup. After an evening of brainstorming they had chosen a new course of action and this was it. A brand-new day, a brand-new plan.

"I guess," Edie grumbled, but before

Kappy could get out of the car, the familiar figure appeared on the porch.

Martha Peachey shaded her eyes and studied the car that had just pulled up in her driveway. "Kathryn King, is that you?" she called.

"Duty calls." Kappy got out of the car and pasted on a smile. "Hi, Martha."

Martha Peachey lived on the other side of Jimmy and Edie. Though they shared a last name, they weren't related. At least not as far back as anyone could remember. Not that it even mattered. Half the Amish in the valley shared the last name of Peachey.

"I thought you were done running all over the place in that terrible car."

Kappy heard Edie chuckle before she shut the door and made her way over to the porch.

"Edie's my friend," Kappy started, then wished she hadn't spoken. No sense in defending herself. Nothing would suit Martha.

"You jumping the fence?" Martha asked.

Kappy resisted the urge to roll her eyes. "No, Martha. I'm not jumping the fence."

"Because if you are, you would need to find someone else to sew our coverings."

"*Jah,* Martha. I know." It was a conversation they'd had before.

"Come on up here and sit with me."

Kappy cast a quick glance at the car where Edie waited, then made her way up the porch steps and settled herself down in one of the waiting chairs. The chairs were mismatched, one straight backed and squatty, the other a beautiful rocker. Martha picked the rocker and waited for Kappy to state the reason for her visit.

"Do you remember Alma's sister, Amelia?"

"Of course I do. Has someone contacted her about poor Alma's death?" Martha clicked her dentures. "Poor thing. So tragic."

"Jah," Kappy murmured.

"What did she say?" Martha asked.

"About what?"

"About her sister's death. You said someone had contacted her."

"No, I —" Kappy pinched the bridge of her nose. "That's kind of what I wanted to talk to you about."

"Me?" She clicked her teeth once again.

"What do you remember about Amelia?"

Martha rocked back and stared at the porch ceiling. "She was a good girl, a little on the heavy side, but all of those Gingerich girls are. Except for Rose. She took after their *dat,* you know."

"Where is Amelia now?"

241

"I wouldn't begin to know. She jumped the fence so far back . . ."

Jumped the fence . . . left the Amish. "When was that?"

"Goodness, let's see that had to be at least forty years ago or better."

That long. So why would Alma be referring to her sister after all this time?

"Does the phrase 'nine babies' mean anything to you?"

"Nine babies?" Martha asked. "Not a thing at all."

Edie sighed in frustration. "That was a complete bust."

"I wouldn't say a complete. We know that Amelia left the Amish."

"Yeah, forty years ago. And didn't we already know that?"

After talking with Martha, they had gone back to Edie's and gathered around the kitchen table to reassess all they knew. It wasn't much.

"Maybe you should look her up on the Internet." Kappy and Edie both turned to look at Jimmy.

As if sensing their eyes on him, he glanced up from the leather leash he was braiding for Judith to wear during the competition. "What?"

"That's a great idea." Edie pushed up from the table and went into the living room to fetch her laptop.

But after a quick search there was . . . "Nothing." Edie sat back in her seat. "No Facebook page, no Twitter, no blog, not even a LinkedIn account."

"I don't know what any of that means."

"It means that Amelia Gingerich left the Amish and disappeared."

"Her name wouldn't be Gingerich if she got married after she left," Jimmy said.

Edie looked at Kappy. She could only shrug and smile. It seemed that Jimmy had all the answers this afternoon.

"That's right. But we don't know what her name might have been," Edie said.

"So it's a dead end."

"I'm afraid so."

"We are not going to make this a habit," Kappy said, adjusting Edie's prayer *kapp* as they walked toward the gathering.

"You think I like this?" Edie pulled at the waistband of her dress, then winced as she was stuck by one of the pins holding it in place. "Ouch." She sucked on the wound, then shot Kappy an offended look. "Your fault."

"My fault? How so?"

"I wouldn't be here if it weren't for you."

Kappy shook her head. "You should just go ahead and admit it. You'd take any chance you got to dress Amish again."

"Untrue on so many levels."

Kappy laughed, then the conversation between them dropped as they entered the crush of people who had come to see Alma Miller laid to rest.

"Keep your eyes and ears open. Surely somebody knows something."

"Got it, boss."

"And try to blend in." With blue-and-pink hair that might be a little difficult. She could only hope and pray that no one looked at Edie closely enough to know who she was. And since she had been back in Blue Sky for the last several months, the chance that someone would recognize her were greater than when they attended Sally June Esh's funeral.

Kappy watched Edie sashay away and resisted the urge to pull her back. This was never going to work. She probably should have come by herself. And if this same thing had happened before Edie Peachey had returned to Blue Sky, Kappy would have come here alone. But since she and Edie had become friends, she had gotten accustomed to having a friend at her side.

Good or bad, right or wrong, there it was.

"Kappy."

She turned as Mary Raber came up behind her. Just the person she wanted to talk to. If anyone knew the latest rumors, it was Mary.

But Mary chatted on about the upcoming festival, the boysenberry pies that would be baked, and a host of other things. Just not what Kappy wanted to talk about.

"What about Emmy Blue? Amelia," Kappy asked. "Did anybody try to contact her about Alma's passing?"

"I don't think so," Mary said.

"Why not? Shouldn't her sister know that she died?"

"Of course, but Emmy Blue herself died years ago."

"What?"

Mary nodded. "And wait until you see what Frannie Lehman brought to the funeral today."

Kappy waited patiently for her to continue.

"Boysenberry pie."

"I'm sure she's just been practicing for the festival."

"Well, I for one think it's shameful."

"Maybe she meant it as a tribute," Kappy mused.

Mary sniffed. "Maybe." But she said no more as Bertha Troyer came up.

"Kappy," Bertha started. "There's a woman over by the barn. Is that Edie Peachey?"

Kappy almost choked. "Why would Edie Peachey be here?" So it wasn't exactly an answer. *When all else fails, change the subject.* "I know a lot of people are wondering what happens to Alma's pie recipe now. As far as I've ever known, Alma was the only one who knew it."

"Rose might know it," Bertha said.

"Of course," Mary said. "Rose would be the logical person to have the recipe. It was a family recipe, right?"

"What about Nancy?" Kappy asked. Nancy lived in Lancaster and had come up for the funeral. She didn't make many trips to the valley, preferring instead the busyness of the touristy towns in Lancaster County.

Just then, Rose herself walked up. She had only caught the tail end of the conversation, but it was enough for her to know what they were talking about. "You've got it all wrong. Emmy Blue and Alma came up with that recipe just after Alma got married. They were the only two who knew it."

■ ■ ■ ■

"Why would she bring a boysenberry pie to a funeral?" Edie asked.

The funeral was over and they were headed home with only a little more information than when they had started.

"It's not like it's unheard of." In fact there were several other pies besides the traditional "funeral" pie made with raisins.

"But boysenberry? It's like she was smearing everyone's nose in it."

"In the pie?"

Edie waved away her surprise. "It's just an expression. It means she was showing off and no one could do anything about it."

"If you say so."

"Did you eat any of it?" Edie asked.

"It was gone by the time I got over there."

"It tasted a lot like Alma's pie. A lot."

"When was the last time you had any of Alma's boysenberry pie?" Kappy asked.

"Before I left."

"That was ten years ago," Kappy exclaimed.

"Alma's pies aren't easily forgotten."

"True dat."

"Are we going there again?" Edie shot her a deadly look.

Kappy laughed, then stopped. "Do you think Frannie has Alma's recipe?"

"I don't know," Edie mused. "But the pies are very much alike."

"Rose Menno said that only Emmy Blue and Alma had the recipe."

"Emmy Blue is dead."

"And so is Alma," Kappy countered.

"But if she wrote it down . . ."

"And her recipe box was stolen . . ." Kappy continued.

"I thought we had agreed that Frannie was innocent."

"I think we agreed that we *wanted* Frannie to be innocent."

They rode along, the only sounds the *clop* of the horse's hooves and the metallic *whir* of the wheels.

"Maybe there's something in the nine babies," Edie pondered.

"Like what?"

"What do we know about the number nine?" Edie asked.

Kappy thought about it a moment. "There are nine fruits of the spirit."

"Right," Edie said. "Love, joy, peace." She ticked each off on her fingers.

"Patience, self-control," Kappy added.

"That's five."

"Uh . . . gentleness."

248

"Six."

"Goodness, faithfulness . . ."

"Kindness," Edie finished triumphantly.

"And what does that have to do with Alma?"

"Other than Alma represents all of those, nothing else that I can see."

Kappy nodded. "Okay, let's file than one away for now. What else about nine?"

Edie shrugged.

"Let's see. The ninth hour is the hour of prayer."

"Okay."

"Jesus died in the ninth hour on the cross."

"Really?" Edie asked.

Kappy shot her a look.

"What?"

"That is something you should know."

Edie nodded. "You're probably right."

"What else?"

"Cats have nine lives."

"And that doesn't have one thing to do with babies."

Edie shook her head. "This is making my head hurt." She reached under her apron and pulled out her cell phone.

"Edie!" Kappy screeched. "You had that with you the entire time?"

"Of course. What if Jimmy needed me?"

"What if it had started to ring? Your cover

would have been blown."

"I had it set to silent." Edie started tapping it, completely dismissing Kappy's concerns.

"What are you doing?"

"I'm looking this up."

"The number nine?"

"Of course." She tapped the screen a couple more times, then fell silent as she started to read to herself.

After a few minutes, she gasped. "Listen to this," she said, then started to read aloud to Kappy. " 'During Viking times, the father had to recognize his newborn baby on the ninth night after birth. The infant was brought to the father and placed on his knee. Then the baby was sprinkled with water and given a name.' That's like baptism. I had no idea Vikings baptized their children."

"And how was Alma supposed to know that? Better yet, why would she care about it?"

"Shhh," Edie shushed and continued to read. " 'Once this happens the baby is officially part of the family and could not be killed without the death being considered murder.' Whoa."

"Interesting but not pertinent. Is there anything else?"

"Is *pertinent* today's word?" Edie asked.

Kappy shot her a little smile. "One from last month. Now, focus."

Edie turned her attention back to her phone. "Uhum . . . May ninth is Europe Day . . . The word November comes from the Latin *novem* meaning nine."

"That's weird," Kappy said. "September is the ninth month."

"Something to do with the Roman calendar."

"September . . ." Kappy pondered the month. "What happens in September?"

"If it had to do with September, why didn't Alma just write that?"

"Why did she write ME for Emmy?"

"Good point."

"Is her birthday in September?" Kappy asked.

"I would know this how?"

"Right." Kappy slowed the carriage, then tugged on the reins to turn the horse onto School Yard Road.

"Finally." Edie sighed. "Buggy travel seems to take forever."

"Only when you're not used to it."

"I don't want to get used to it."

Kappy laughed. "If nine means September, then nine babies could be September babies, right?"

"Sure, but what is September babies? Sounds like a rock band."

"I'm pretty certain Alma didn't listen to rock and roll music."

"So she could be talking about babies who were born in September."

"Maybe. But Alma didn't have any children, did she?"

"Again, I know this how?"

"Maybe we should talk to Martha again."

"Maybe we should go home and get my car first."

Kappy shot her a look.

"What? We have to drive right past there."

"We are not stopping."

But in the end, they stopped to tell Jimmy where they were going, and he ended up in the buggy with them, riding down to their neighbor's house.

"It's about time I saw you in a buggy, Kathryn." Martha let the door slam behind her as she came out onto the porch.

"Hi, Martha." Kappy climbed down from the buggy, with Jimmy close behind. Edie got out a little more slowly, still tugging on her Amish clothing.

"Did you see my sister? She's dressed Amish." Jimmy bounded up to Martha like an overgrown puppy.

"You coming back to this side of the fence?"

"Hardly."

"Hmm." Martha clicked her teeth. "That means I can't talk to you."

"You're talking to me — ow!" Edie broke off as Kappy stepped on her foot. Hard.

"Martha," Kappy started, "is there anything significant about September babies?"

"I would say that September babies are the absolute best babies there are."

Kappy and Edie shared a quick look.

"And why is that?" Kappy asked.

"Because I'm one."

"Is it a club or something?"

Martha chuckled. "If you're talking about a club, then I wasn't aware of one. I was just born in September."

"What about any significant births in September?" Edie asked.

Martha turned to Kappy, waiting for her to repeat the question so she could answer it.

Kappy obliged, Edie rolled her eyes, and Martha started pondering.

"There was a time when two sets of twins were born in the same month. But that was October. Not September."

"Maybe something involving Alma Miller and her sisters . . ."

"Moreover, her sister Emmy Blue," Edie said.

Martha patiently waited for Kappy to repeat.

"Amelia," Kappy supplied. "Was there anything about the two of them, and babies in the month of September?" It was a long shot. Alma didn't have any children. Everyone in Blue Sky knew that.

Martha tapped the edge of her chin, then twirled the tied string of her prayer *kapp* around the end of one finger. "There was one year. Heavens, that was so long ago. Nigh on fifty years," she mused. "I had almost forgotten about it."

"About what?" Kappy coaxed.

"That September. *Jah,* I'm pretty sure it was September, Emmy Blue and Alma had their babies."

Kappy shot a quick look at Edie, knowing they were thinking the same thing: Alma didn't have any children.

"But . . ." Kappy stuttered, then finally found the words. "I didn't think Alma had any children."

Martha clicked her teeth. "She didn't have any children who *lived.*"

Another look.

"Are you saying that Alma had a child that died?"

"Stillborn." Martha nodded.

"In September?" Kappy asked.

"Jah."

"And that same year, in September, Emmy Blue had a baby?"

"Maybe we should sit awhile. This may take a bit." Martha hobbled back to the porch without waiting to see if anyone followed. She settled down into her rocking chair.

Having no choice, Edie and Kappy followed.

"Let me see now . . ." Martha rocked back as she tried to remember. "It was a while back."

They knew that, of course, but Kappy didn't want to question Martha and make her lose her train of thought.

"Alma and Samuel had just gotten married. Amelia had joined the church, but everyone knew her heart wasn't in it. She just did it because of their father. So nobody was really surprised when she left. Except for their father. He was shocked. Alma got pregnant and the baby died. Amelia came back to see her, and she was pregnant. She had her baby while she was trying to nurse her sister's spirit. Alma was told that she would never have children. That was at the first of September, Amelia's baby was born

255

at the end. I remember this because my birthday is in the middle, the sixteenth.

"She wasn't married then, you know, but I think she eventually married the father. After Alma got back on her feet, Amelia went back to whatever life she had built for herself.

"Of course she was shunned. Like other people we know." She shot a look in Edie's direction.

"Did she have any more children?"

"Maybe. I don't know. I didn't hear anything about her. I figure Alma kept in touch. They were too close to let even the *Ordnung* keep them apart. But I don't know any details. Weren't none of my business."

"Did she have a boy or a girl?"

Martha smiled. "They both had girls."

"We've got to tell Jack." Kappy's heart was pounding with excitement. Part of the mystery had been solved.

"Why? This is nothing."

"Maybe to us. But I'm sure he has more to work with."

Edie shook her head.

"Why don't you want to see Jack?" Kappy asked.

"I want to see Jack," Jimmy said from the back seat.

"You just want cake," Edie grumbled. "And you didn't say anything about inviting him to supper."

"I didn't say anything about *not* inviting him to supper, either," Kappy countered.

"What's the matter with cake?" Jimmy asked.

"Come on," Kappy said. "You know you love having Jack over to eat." Not that she would ever admit it.

"Fine." She sighed. "But you can call him while I change clothes."

"Deal," Kappy said with a laugh. "But you have to wear normal Edie clothes."

"What's that supposed to mean?"

"You can't wear your 'English soccer mom' outfits."

Edie harrumphed. "What do you know about soccer moms?"

"Enough to know you don't need to dress like one."

A knock sounded on the door almost two hours later. Kappy peeked out of the kitchen as Jimmy raced down the stairs.

"That's Jack! That's Jack! That's Jack!" He jumped over the last three steps, landed, stumbled, then continued his lunge for the door.

He flung it open and there stood . . .

Frannie Lehman's daughters.

"Is Kappy here?" one of them asked.

"Awh . . ." Jimmy tried to not look so disappointed. But the lack of expression was hard for him. "Hi," he grumbled, stepping back and allowing them to enter. "Kappy, some girls from the bakery are here to see you."

She came out of the kitchen wiping her hands on her apron. "Susie, Amanda, how did you know where to find me?"

Susie gave a small shrug. "We remembered that you two came into the bakery together. When you didn't answer your door, we decided to check here."

"I'm glad you did. What can I do for you?" she asked.

"We need your help. Yours and . . . Edie's."

"Edie's?" Kappy raised her brows in surprise.

"We know Edie's shunned," Susie said, twisting her hands together. "This is important."

"Come sit down." Edie gestured toward the kitchen table. It had been set for their supper with Jack.

"Are you expecting company?"

"In a bit. I want to hear what you have to say," Edie said. Kappy wondered if she was so willing to postpone dinner simply because she was happy that someone Amish was speaking to her.

"We're worried about *Mamm*," Susie said.

"Now that Alma has passed," Amanda's voice wavered as she spoke, "we're afraid that the police will arrest her. The bakery does good for itself, but without her . . ."

"And what would Helen do?" Susie asked, referring to their youngest sister. "She's not even eleven."

"We need our mother," Amanda said. "We would be lost without her."

Edie's forehead crumpled into a crinkly frown. "What do you think we can do?"

"Well, everyone knows that you found Ruth's killer." Susie's voice dropped as she said the last word. "I'm sorry."

"It's okay," Edie said, but Kappy saw the sheen of tears in her eyes. She blinked them away and waved a hand for Susie to continue.

"And we know that you were instrumental in helping the police find who ran Sally June Esh off the road."

"What Susie is trying to say is without you two, the real killers might have never been caught."

"I helped, too. Some . . ." Jimmy said.

"The three of you," Amanda corrected with a sweet smile in Jimmy's direction.

"And we would like your help in finding out who killed Alma."

"For *Mamm,*" Susie said.

"Why do you think the police will blame your mother?" Edie asked.

"Seven failed pie championships, *Mamm*'s new pie recipe, the missing recipe box."

"I never saw mention of that in the paper," Kappy said. "How did you know about that?"

"We're Amish, remember? That's all we have to do is talk about one other."

"True dat," Edie muttered.

Kappy acted like she was going to pinch her, but Edie moved her arm out of reach.

"I'm not sure what we can do," Kappy said.

"Anything would help," Amanda said.

"There is one more thing," Susie added after a brief pause. "*Mamm* was seen coming out of the hospital the day Alma died."

"She said she had been to visit another friend, but . . . it doesn't look good, does it?"

As Amanda said the last word, a knock sounded at the door.

"That must be your company," Susie said.

"We'll be going." They stood and hurried for the door, almost apologetic to have come at all. But Kappy could feel for them. They were afraid for their mother. Afraid that she would get arrested, but before they said their goodbyes, Kappy forgot to ask one small thing: Did they think their mother was guilty?

Amanda and Susie hurried past Jack with hardly a look at his swarthy features. Kappy wondered if they were merely in a hurry or if they were intent on hiding as much as they could.

"Who were they?" Jack asked as they flew by and climbed into their buggy.

Kappy hesitated a moment, unsure if she should tell the truth or lie. In the end, she chose the truth. "Frannie Lehman's daughters."

"Hey, Jack," Jimmy called.

"The baker?" he asked as he handed the large bowl to Edie. "Hi, Jimmy."

"What's this?" Edie asked, turning it this way and that as if staring through the bottom of the bowl would give her an answer.

"Dessert. Candy bar pie. There wasn't time for much more."

Wasn't time? But Kappy didn't ask.

"How is there a pie in a bowl?"

He shrugged. "I don't know why they call it a pie at all. It has cake in it."

"Where'd you get this?" Edie asked, still trying to examine it. From what Kappy could see, it was more like a trifle than a pie, but if Jack wanted to call it a pie that was all right with her.

"At that little shop down on . . . what's that smell?" He tipped his head back and sniffed the air.

"That's lasagna," Edie said proudly, but she left out the part that it was the freezer kind and vegetarian. Kappy supposed it didn't matter, she had a feeling that Jack was merely trying to change the subject. But why?

"Thanks for inviting me over tonight." Jack smiled.

"We wanted to talk to you about something," Kappy said. "But it can wait until we all sit down. If we start talking about this now, we might all starve before we get it straightened out."

To Jack's credit he didn't bat an eye over the vegetarian part of the meal plan, but he was surprised to see all the red sauce.

"Have you gotten over your aversion to red foods?" Jack asked.

"Not really," Jimmy said. "But Edie said that if wasn't going to eat meat, then I had to eat more red things and vegetables." He made a face. "So I'm trying. Plus, Kappy is right, if I close my eyes, then all the food is the same color."

He closed his eyes and demonstrated, taking a bite of his food. Okay, so it was a small bite, but as far as Kappy was concerned that was a start. She was fairly certain Edie felt the same.

"What's this big news you want to tell me?" Jack asked about halfway through their meal.

Kappy was surprised Edie had held out that long.

"We found out what the message in the flour means," Edie said. What she had gone back to in dress, she made up for in demeanor. Tonight she looked a little more like the real Edie, lime-green jeans, black-and-white-striped shirt, and cherry-red flats. None of it matched her pastel hair. But she wasn't the same old bubbly Edie. She was on the reserved side, almost quiet. As far as Kappy was concerned it was a bit unnerving.

"The message Alma Miller left in the flour?"

"That's right. Tell him about it, Kappy."

Kappy blinked at her friend, then cleared her throat. "After talking to a few older members of our district, we believe that nine babies means babies born in September."

Jack's eyes widened. "Okay," he said slowly.

"ME blue is what they called Alma's sister, Amelia. Emmy Blue."

"Why blue?" Jack asked.

Kappy shrugged. "I'm not certain, but I believe it was because she had such beautiful blue eyes. Like Alma herself has . . . had."

"What do babies born in September have to do with it?"

"That's the part we aren't really sure about. But we wanted to tell you. Maybe you'll be able to figure it out."

"Of course Jack will figure it out. He's a detective. Right, Jack?"

"Of course," he replied but with much less conviction than Jimmy.

"Here's what we know. Alma and her sister both had babies in September. Alma had her baby at the beginning of the month, Amelia at the end. Alma's baby died; Amelia returned to the English world with hers."

"Where's Amelia now?" he asked.

"Dead." Kappy frowned. "Just like her sister."

Kappy could almost see the thoughts turning over in his mind.

Where's Amelia's daughter? Why is she important? Was she the one who attacked

Alma and why?

Kappy was certain, the information they just handed him was less help than they had intended.

CHAPTER 13

In the days leading up to the festival, the atmosphere in Blue Sky was something akin to hushed excitement. Everyone was waiting for the big pie bake off, but it was sad to know that the queen of pies wouldn't be there this year.

Yet there was more to the festival. Jimmy was preparing his bunny, grooming Judith's coat and making sure that he kept her feet clean. He wanted her to be as beautiful as she could be for the competition. Edie had told Kappy that she caught Jimmy with Judith in his room. She didn't have the heart to make him take the bunny back outside. He had worked so hard for the competition that she wanted him to have every advantage possible, even if it was nothing that would likely make a difference.

Saturday morning dawned bright, with a crisp nip in the breeze, the perfect fall day to begin the fall festival. A sense of expectancy hung in the air. Kappy couldn't tell if it was just the pure, sweet excitement of the upcoming event, or if everyone in Blue Sky was holding their breath to see when the next shoe would drop.

"What time is the judging for the small animals?" Kappy asked as they headed toward the festival. Somehow she had managed to talk Edie into taking her buggy. It was just another form of proof that Edie had something pressing on her mind. Kappy just didn't know if it had something to do with Jack Jones, or Jimmy's entry.

"We have to be there at ten on the dot, the man said." Jimmy patted the small carrier where he had stashed his precious Judith. It was one of his mother's puppy carriers, a soft-sided royal-blue nylon bag with mesh windows on both sides and in the front. A large zipper kept it closed, but Kappy could see Judith's twitching white nose through the front. She seemed not to mind traveling in the least.

"The pie-baking competition starts right after that at eleven," Kappy said. "They're running it the same this year as always. They'll bake their pies, sit them out to cool and allow people to look at their creative crusts, then at three the taste judging will begin."

"Perfect," Edie said. "That will give us plenty of time to get from Jimmy's booth to the pie booth."

"Can we walk around while the pies are cooking?" Jimmy asked.

"What are you going to do with Judith?" Edie wanted to know.

Jimmy patted the carrier once again. "She doesn't seem to mind being in here."

Edie shook her head. "She'll have to go to the bathroom, and she'll need to eat. You can't keep her in there for hours at a time."

Jimmy frowned. "You're right. Maybe I can drive the buggy back to the house and take her home."

Kappy saw the hesitation whether Edie realized she had paused or not. It was as if she was thinking over the request. "Jimmy, that's not a good idea with all the traffic today."

"I can do it," Kappy said. "Jimmy can ride with me, and we'll take Judith home, then meet you back here before the taste judging."

"That's fine."

And Kappy had to wonder if Edie was about to cave and give Jimmy a bit more freedom. Only time would tell.

They turned their buggy over to the young men who were parking them. They took their number, and allowed the boys to do their job, arranging the carriages and turning the horses out in the pastures. Both had a matching number to the one on the card they gave Kappy in order to make sure that the correct horse went with the correct buggy and got back to the correct owner at the end of the day.

The festival was the same as it had been every year, but somehow it managed to maintain its level of wonderment for Kappy. Jimmy, too. And Kappy could tell that Edie was excited to be back.

As far as festivals went, Kappy was certain there were bigger and better, but this one seemed to suit Blue Sky just fine. Down the midway were places to eat. Local restaurants had small cook shacks set up to feed the masses. Frank's IOP and Daisy's Deli, even Blue Sky Baked Goods and Frannie's Bakery had booths to sell premade goods. Other treats included pretzels and of course stuffed pretzels, pickles on a stick, and the ever-popular corndogs. At the end of the row, food truck owners had parked their rigs and were ready for the masses. Street tacos, fried everything, the all-American hamburger, and country barbecue, just to name a few.

"Let's get you checked in," Edie said to

Jimmy. "Then we can get something to drink while we wait for the judging to begin."

Jimmy nodded but swallowed hard. Kappy knew he was nervous. But she wasn't sure if it was because this was his first time doing something like this or if he had his hopes set on winning. She hoped it was the first thing. Not that Judith wasn't a beautiful rabbit. There was usually a lot of competition in his category. A great many of the local farm kids had animals registered.

A row of small pens had been constructed and filled with hay for the comfort of the animals.

"That's good, *jah*?" Jimmy crooned as he placed his bunny in the small pen. "You need lots of hay in your diet. So eat up."

Kappy and Edie stood back as Jimmy took his place beside his pen and waited for the judging to begin. Not only had he been meticulous in Judith's grooming, he had paid extra attention to his own. His neatly tucked-in shirt was clean and without stains, his pants the least worn in the knees of any that he had. His face was scrubbed clean and he had taken some sort of hair product to his cowlick. He had managed to get it to lay down but at the price of it looking like he had glued it to the rest of his hair.

"Oh." Edie bounced on her toes as the judges started down the aisle of small animals under fifteen pounds. She had the fingers on both hands crossed and danced around as if she had to go to the bathroom.

"It's going to be okay," Kappy said, tugging on her elbow to get her to settle down. "Win or lose, he just wanted to compete."

"There are some good animals over there."

And there were. One kid had a large, extra fuzzy cat that Kappy thought was called a Persian, but she wasn't certain. As large as the creature was, Kappy wondered if it actually made it under the fifteen-pound limit. Another had a fat hamster, and even another had a miniature pig.

From time to time Kappy saw Jimmy's gaze stray to the sweet pink creature. She had to admit it was adorable and she could see why Jimmy wanted one. Maybe now, once he had proved some of his maturity with the contest, Edie would consider a pig.

Maybe Kappy was just a pushover when it came to Jimmy, but she saw no harm in letting him have as many animals as he could feed. He took care of them and he loved them. She wondered if perhaps they were a substitute for the family he had lost.

"There's the judge." Edie released her crossed fingers and grabbed Kappy's hand.

"Easy," she said as Edie squeezed. "I have to sew *kapps* with these hands."

"Sorry," Edie said, but she didn't release Kappy's fingers or loosen her own grip.

As they watched, Jimmy nodded, then reached into the pen and pulled Judith out. He cradled her in his hands, gently turning her this way and that so the judges could see her from all angles. He held her up so they could see the bottom of her feet. Then they pointed her long ears upward and watched them fall back into place.

"He's doing good," Edie said.

Jimmy placed Judith back into her pen, then shook the judges' hands before taking his place next to the pen. Kappy blinked. Jimmy, who hated being touched voluntarily, shook hands with three strangers. Well, two strangers, the third judge was the county sheriff and though Jimmy might not know him personally, he had spent nearly two weeks in the county jail not so long ago.

When the judges turned their attention to the next entrant, Jimmy caught Kappy and Edie's attention. He shot them a big smile and a thumbs-up. He thought he'd done a good job and that was a big accomplishment.

Once all the animals had been judged and their scores tallied, the winners were announced. Jimmy and Judith came in third behind the fuzzy cat and the mini pig.

"I'm never going to hear the end of it about a pig now, am I?" But Edie wore a grin that stretched from ear to ear. Kappy didn't think she had seen her smile like that the whole time she had been back in Blue Sky.

"Probably not."

A few minutes later, Jimmy had Judith packed away in her carrier. He bounded over to them, the white ribbon pinned to his chest. "I did it!" he cried. "I won."

"That you did," Edie said.

"Way to go." Kappy cried, then Jimmy launched himself at them wrapping his arms around them both.

"Oof," Edie groaned.

"Judith," Kappy managed to squeak. She hated to break up what was essentially a breakthrough for him, but win or not, he would be devastated if he hurt his bunny.

"Oh, sorry." He pulled away, still grinning.

Kappy pretended not to notice as Edie wiped the tears from her eyes.

"You ready to run your prize-winning rabbit back home?" Kappy asked.

Jimmy beamed. "Can I wear my ribbon

all day?"

"You bet," Edie said. "You bet."

Once Judith was safely back in her hutch at the Peachey farm and Kappy and Jimmy were back at the festival, they met up with Edie at the pie competition arena.

"What'd we miss?" Kappy asked as she came up next to her friend.

"Can I go look at the horses?" Jimmy asked.

"Yes," Edie said. "Just be careful. You know how some horses can be."

"Jah." He nodded. "And I've got my necklace if something happens." He pulled the small device out from under his shirt to show her. Then he tucked it back inside.

"Come back here by three," Edie said. "Can you find out what time it is?" she asked.

"Of course, I'll just ask somebody." Jimmy shot her a look like it was the dumbest question ever asked in the history of the world.

He gave them a quick wave and disappeared in the crowd.

"Be safe," Edie whispered.

"He's going to be fine. He's almost twenty-one years old."

"I know but in so many ways he's just a child."

"And that's one of the things that makes him so special and so lovable."

"*Mamm* would come back and kill me if I let anything happen to him."

Kappy shook her head. "First of all, that is entirely impossible, second, an Amish woman ex or not should not be talking like that, and third, nothing is going to happen to him."

"Yeah, you're right."

"Now tell me what I missed."

"Not much. Greta Menno entered the competition in Alma Miller's place."

Of course. Greta was Rose's daughter, and niece to Alma the pie queen, but that didn't mean that she could bake. Perhaps the family — mainly Rose — wanted to be represented at the competition.

They hadn't put their pies in the ovens yet. Kappy and Edie watched as the judges went from booth to booth examining the unfinished products and asking questions.

The contestants had brought the pie filing already mixed from home. That way everyone's secret ingredients could remain secret. Once they were at their booths, they had to mix up their pie crusts, construct their pies, and bake them in the ovens that had been brought in for this very competition.

Bobbie Jean Hawkins walked with the

other judges but somehow managed to stand out. It wasn't that she wore anything spectacular. In fact, her outfit was about as fancy and outlandish as Edie's soccer mom getup. Which was none. Her brown hair showed copper highlights in the midday sun and her eyes still sparkled as they had the first time Kappy had seen her. There was nothing odd or outstanding about Bobby Jean Hawkins. But that sense of familiarity stole over Kappy once again. The feeling was so intense she shivered.

"You okay?" Edie leaned close when she spoke as if she didn't want anyone to overhear. The crowd was incredibly quiet, like those golf games Kappy had seen on the televisions in Walmart. Everything was whispered and hushed. She figured it was because it helped the men golf better, but this crowd was silent trying to catch any hint of what the judges were writing down, what they thought about the pies at this point, and if they already had a favorite on their list.

"*Jah,* just . . ." She didn't want to go through it again, all that talk about déjà vu, though she didn't think that was the problem at all. It wasn't that she felt like she had been here before. She felt like she had met Bobbie Jean Hawkins. But where? It simply wasn't possible.

Maybe Bobbie Jean just looked like someone else Kappy knew. Didn't everyone have a doppelganger? That was today's word. And it sure fit better then déjà vu.

"Just what?" Edie asked.

"It's just exciting," she lied. It was better than having to explain something she had no idea what it even was.

Once the pies went into the oven, the crowd thinned a bit. The pies wouldn't take very long to cook, and some people were reluctant to give up their prime spot to watch the exciting pie bake off reaction. Most of these wore I ♥ BOBBIE JEAN badges on their clothing. Kappy shook her head, wondering where this large following for the judges had started and then she remembered. People thought that Mrs. O'Malley's Pies was looking for new recipes. Perhaps they were hoping that if something didn't happen with the boysenberry pie winner, Bobbie Jean might consider their own apple, pecan, or even sweet potato. Anything was possible, Kappy supposed.

The contestants seemed so very serious. Especially for pie. Diana Chamberland wore a T-shirt from her bakery and a baseball cap with her ponytail spilling out the back. Her smile was confident and infectious. Frannie

Lehman had on her usual frown with to-day's black dress and apron. Hair tightly pulled back and firmly secured. Not one strand out of place as if none would dare defy her. The other bakers were somewhere in between.

"Hey." The whispered greeting behind them had them both whirling around to see who it was.

"Jack." Edie pressed a hand to her heart. "You scared the life out of me."

"I certainly hope not."

"What are you doing here?" Kappy asked. "Are you on duty or just out enjoying your-self?"

"On duty as always." Now that they had a homicide on their hands. Well, he had one on his hands, so to speak.

"Not much longer and they'll be taking them out of the ovens."

"We were going to stay until that time, then walk around until the tasting at three."

"I'm hoping to get me a piece of that boysenberry." He rubbed his flat stomach.

"They're all boysenberry," Edie dryly reminded him.

"Okay, then Frannie's. I've heard that she's got a new recipe that's out of this world."

"I wonder if that's what she had at the

278

funeral," Edie mused.

"She brought a boysenberry pie to the funeral?" Jack asked. "Alma Miller's funeral?"

"Exactly."

"What was it like?"

"Just like Alma's," Edie said. "To the best I can remember anyway. I've been reminded that I haven't had an Alma Miller pie in ten years."

Jack turned to Kappy for confirmation. "I have no idea," she said. "I didn't have a piece at the funeral."

"When was the last time that you had a piece of her boysenberry pie?"

"A couple of months, I guess."

Jack looked over to the cooling table where the pies were being placed for the next to the last round of judging. Then he checked his watch. "We've got almost two hours before we'll be able to try any of that pie."

"She carries them in her bakery."

"Perfect idea." He grabbed Kappy by the wrist and started tugging her through the crowd.

"Wait," she cried. "Where are we going?"

"To Frannie's Bakery to get a boysenberry pie."

■ ■ ■ ■

"See, this way we can taste the pie before they start the judging." Jack nodded as if that explained everything. They had taken his police car over to Frannie's and bought the pie from Susie, who claimed they had drawn lots to see who minded the shop. She had lost and therefore had to work the first day of the festival. Kappy had a feeling Susie got the short end of the stick often when it came to matters of family.

"Why do we need to taste this pie again?" she asked.

They had managed to find Jimmy before leaving the festival grounds. He was still with the pigs — imagine that! — and they told him to stay put and they would be right back. Kappy could tell that Edie was reluctant to leave him but unwilling to let her and Jack go alone. In the end, she allowed Jimmy the freedom and hopped in the car.

"We're going to see how close the recipe is to Alma Miller's." Jack was serious as he drove. His expression was so intense underneath that dark stubble of his that he looked almost sinister.

"We?" Kappy asked from her place in the back seat.

"Well, you," he corrected. "You know what the pie's supposed to taste like."

"What's that going to prove?" Kappy did not understand.

"If the pie is the same recipe, then it's more than likely that the killer acquired it when they took Alma's recipe box."

"And that Frannie Lehman is the killer?" Kappy caught Edie's gaze.

"She's been our top suspect since day one."

But Kappy didn't want Frannie to be guilty. The woman worked hard, she trusted God and her community. She didn't think Frannie had it in her to harm another, regardless of rivalries and jealousies and every other weed that could thrive in a small garden such as Blue Sky.

But Frannie had a secret that Kappy didn't think the police knew. Frannie had been at the hospital the day Alma died. And that, she had to admit, did look suspicious.

As if reading her thoughts, Edie gave a tiny shake of her head. They couldn't tell Jack about Frannie going to the hospital on the day Alma died. It was simply too suspect.

Kappy had read in the paper that Alma's autopsy showed that someone had poisoned her with bleach. She herself had read enough mysteries to know that a syringe full on bleach injected into an IV line was enough to kill. And seeing as how the hospital used bleach to clean, anyone could have done it. Everyone had access. All they had to do was wait until backs were turned. Until the loved ones and support teams who were waiting left to get something to eat. A crime like that didn't take long.

"What if Frannie just managed to uncover Alma's pie secrets?" After all, how many tricks to baking a pie were there? There couldn't be that many.

"That's doubtful."

"Why?" Edie asked. "She's worked on it for years."

"And she just happened to discover it right after the baker dies and her recipe box disappears."

"I know it might look suspicious, but it's possible. What about the quilt?" Kappy asked. "How does that play in?"

Jack tapped the side of his thumb on the steering wheel. "I figure the vic took it off the bed, probably washed it, and stuck it in a closet instead of putting it back. The husband just hasn't found where she stashed it yet."

It was possible, but that didn't sound like Alma Miller at all. She would have taken that quilt down from the line and put it right back on the bed. That is, if she had washed it in the first place. The whole thing was just a theory.

"But if Frannie made up her own version of Alma's pie, then that means the person who attacked Alma is still out there seeking what they wanted: her recipe for boysenberry pie."

"Or they got it when they stole the recipe box."

Kappy shook her head. "According to her sister, Alma never wrote it down. Now that she's gone the pie recipe is gone with her."

"Which means," Edie joined in, "Frannie is in danger. The person who attacked Alma then snuck into her hospital room to finish off the job still doesn't have the recipe."

Kappy and Edie executed a high five, each grinning. They had done it. They had just kept Frannie Lehman out of jail.

"It doesn't always work that way," Jack said. "And if this pie tastes like Alma's, then the evidence points to Frannie."

Okay. Maybe not.

They rode in silence back to the festival. Kappy felt like she was on a funeral march as she walked the pie down to where the competition was being held. A few people were still milling around, but the crowd had mostly dispersed. Everyone would be back in an hour or so to see the judging.

"Right here is fine." Jack gestured toward a small bench off to one side. With so many people about, it was a miracle that no one was sitting there. Or maybe an omen.

Jack got a knife and fork from a nearby food vendor and presented them to Kappy. She hesitated before accepting the plastic utensils. She was about to taste this pie and the outcome could put someone in jail. The pressure was staggering. How could she say yes and watch as they arrested Frannie Lehman? How could she lie and say the pie was not the same as Alma's?

Or she could taste it and trust God that it would come out the way it was supposed to.

She sliced the pie as best she could with the small knife but ended up scooping a bite out of the middle. Her hand shook as she raised the fork to her mouth. *Lord, please let this be Your will,* she prayed, then took the bite.

The pie was tangy, sweet, and familiar. And just like Alma Miller's.

Kappy's heart fell, and her stomach clenched. How strange to eat something so wonderful, knowing that if she said as much someone was going to jail. A someone that she thought and hoped was innocent.

She swallowed, coughed a bit, then recovered. Dragging this out wouldn't help Frannie at all.

"Well?" Jack asked.

"It tastes just like Alma's."

"I knew it." Jack clenched a fist in victory. "Thanks, Kappy."

She couldn't respond.

Jack turned away as if to leave. "Hang on to that pie for me," he said.

He wasn't having any trouble executing his job. He believed Frannie was guilty, and he was going to arrest her.

Edie laid one hand on his arm, effectively stopping him with the light touch. "She's not going anywhere," she said. "Can you wait until after the judging?"

He stopped, seemed to think it over. "If she wins, it will be with someone else's pie recipe."

"You don't know that for certain."

"I have good cause to believe it's true."

"Please," Edie said. "Win or lose, you can arrest her after the judging. If she is innocent, then she deserves to have her moment in the spotlight."

It seemed Jack had a soft streak after all. But Kappy and Edie had suspected from the start.

"Fine." He made his voice gruff, as if they were annoying him. Kappy didn't believe it for a moment. "But you stay with me and no tipping her off," he finished.

They nodded. What choice did they have?

By the time three o'clock rolled around, Kappy was a nervous wreck. She wanted Frannie to win so badly. And those were words she never thought would cross her mind. But there they were.

The judges arrived back at the cooling tables. Each pie had been placed on a table with the baker standing nearby. The judges walked around them, noting their appearance. Was the crust golden brown? Had the filling oozed out the side or the vent cuts? Had they been creative in their overall presentation? Some pies had lattice tops while others used the full crust. Kappy knew that it took longer, but she liked the look of the lattice. Something about peering into the pie and seeing all that beautiful fruit baked in. Frannie's pie had a lattice crust. Just another point for her.

After they made their marks on appearance, they cut a piece and passed it around, each judge taking a bite out of the pie. Just one bite. It was all held in the balance of one small taste.

With Alma Miller out of the competition, everyone knew it would come down to Diana Chamberland and Frannie Lehman. Kappy knew Frannie's pie tasted good. Well, it did if it tasted anything like the one they had bought at the bakery. Diana Chamberland's pie was perhaps the most creative. She had used a cutter and her top crust had little hearts cut out all around the edge. In the center was another, larger heart, cute and sweet. Frannie might win on taste, but Diana had them all on creativity.

Everyone held their breath when the judges got to Frannie's table. After all these years of entering this competition, all the years of trying and baking only to come in second, Frannie looked nervous as the judges examined her pie and made their notes.

Kappy leaned into Jack. "Why would a woman who stole the blue-ribbon-winning pie recipe be nervous?" She gestured toward Frannie, who had her hands clasped in front of her as she shifted ever so slightly from side to side.

"Because she knows that when they taste her pie everyone is going to know that she stole the recipe."

Kappy rolled her eyes, but he could have a point. If she thought Frannie was guilty.

Which she didn't.

After looking at all the pies and then tasting them, the judges sat down at a small table and tallied scores. Somehow in the middle of a festival, the whole place grew quiet. Kappy studied each of the judges. There were five in all — Delilah Swanson, the preacher's wife; Devlin Franks, who managed the Super Saver grocery store, the Widow Kate, who had been a judge for as long as Kappy could remember; and Joan the Mennonite, who lived on the other side of Jacks Mountain and sold handmade candy in the smaller stores like Hiram's Sundries and Sweets. Normally the fifth judge was the mayor, but she had given up her place this year in order to make room for Bobbie Jean Hawkins.

It seemed to take forever for the judges to tally the scores. The crowd was getting a bit antsy, anxious to see who would win this year.

Finally, Bobbie Jean Hawkins wrote everything on a sheet of paper and handed it off to the mayor.

Deb McDonald opened the folded piece of paper, read what it said to herself, then stepped to the microphone. Her expression never changed.

"Remind me never to play poker with

her," Edie said.

Kappy frowned. "What?"

Jack shushed them.

Kappy knew he was just waiting for the winners to be announced so he could arrest Frannie Lehman.

She also knew that Frannie wasn't guilty and that made it all the harder to stand there.

"I know you don't want me to stand up here talking, so let's get to the good stuff. Honorable Mention goes to Sandy Johnson." Everyone clapped as a young English woman stepped forward to receive her yellow ribbon. Kappy thought she recognized her as one of the bakers at the Super Saver.

"Third prize belongs to Diana Chamberland." The Blue Sky baker stepped forward to accept her white ribbon. She gave the crowd a tight smile as they clapped for her. It was obvious to Kappy that she thought she should have scored higher.

"Our second-place winner is Nancy Esh."

The crowd exploded. At the least the Amish people let loose. It was good to see Nancy out and about, moving on after losing her daughter in the summer.

Nancy smiled and accepted the red ribbon, then stood to one side as the crowd hushed.

"I suppose this is the moment that you have all been waiting for?"

"Yes!" someone shouted.

"Get on with it," someone else called.

Deb shot them both her tolerant politician's smile.

"And the winner of this year's Pie Bake Competition is Frannie Lehman."

Kappy wasn't positive but she thought she heard as many boos as cheers of "good job" and "way to go." It was sad really, so many people had already judged her not knowing even half the facts. And what would those Negative Natalies say when Jack Jones arrested Frannie for Alma's murder? She wasn't sure she could stay around and witness it.

But for now, Frannie was all smiles as they pinned the blue ribbon to her apron strap. She looked a little stunned as if she had waited for this moment for so long and now that it was here, it didn't feel real. Or maybe the joy of winning without Alma as her competition was bittersweet.

"Thank you," Frannie said when the cheers — both good and bad — calmed down. "I would like to dedicate this win to my longtime rival and still dear friend, Alma Miller. No one could say that Alma and I didn't have our difference, but not having her here today . . ." She stopped and wiped the tears from her eyes. "Well, I hope there are bushels of boysenberries where you are, Alma, and I hope you can bake to your heart's content." She bowed her head in reverence or prayer, then stepped away from the microphone.

A man approached her with a camera, but Deb McDonald shooed him away. He must have been new to Blue Sky. Something in the motion drew Kappy's attention to Bobbie Jean Hawkins. Or maybe it was because she took that moment to approach Frannie.

The image of someone else flashed before her eyes as Kappy watched Bobbie Jean. The sense of familiarity became a sinking feeling of . . . almost dread. She really needed to remember why Bobbie Jean looked so familiar. Somehow it was important. She just knew it. But like all the times when she tried really hard to think of something specific, the harder she thought about it the more elusive the memory became.

Elusive. That was tomorrow's word.

And what in the world was she doing thinking about her calendar when Jack Jones was about to arrest Frannie for a crime she didn't commit?

He had already moved into place, and her heart hurt for this member of their community. Frannie had finally achieved her goal, as it was, and now that sense of happiness was about to be shattered.

Kappy watched, knuckles pressed against her mouth as Jack approached Frannie. He moved in close, and she started to back away. He cupped her elbow to stop her, then leaned in to tell her the news. Her eyes went wide, her mouth formed a soundless *O,* and all the color drained from her face.

Jack continued to talk to her, it seemed where no one else could hear. Kappy supposed they couldn't. No one was turning around and staring at the two of them or pointing and laughing at Frannie's misery. And that was good. At least he had spared her that.

He said something else and she nodded, slowly at first then with more assurance.

Jack nodded in response, then with his hand on her elbow he escorted her from the premises. A few heads turned as they walked away together. They looked a little strange side by side, a frowny Amish woman with a blue ribbon fluttering on her chest and a tall, rumpled man with hair as dark as pitch and a stubbly growth of beard to match.

It wouldn't be long before people started

asking questions about where they went. Someone would know, or someone else would make up whatever they wanted the rumor to be, and the "news" would be all over town before suppertime.

CHAPTER 14

"I just don't understand how he could arrest her." Edie stomped around her kitchen forcefully laying out three pieces of bread, then smacking cheese on top of the slices. "Did he not listen to anything we said?"

It was a trick question, and Kappy wasn't about to answer it. And the sandwiches Edie was so violently putting together? Kappy was certain there was no hope for them, either.

But she had prayed for Frannie. She wanted to have hope, because deep in her heart she knew that Frannie was innocent.

"I think he knew that Frannie had been to the hospital that day."

Edie whirled around. "Did you tell him?" She pointed the butter knife she had been using to spread mustard at Kappy. "I know I didn't."

"Anyone could have told him. Or it could have been a matter of security cameras.

They know who comes in and who goes out. That sort of thing isn't kept secret any longer."

Edie turned back to the sandwiches. "Can we get a hold of this footage? Maybe we'll see something he didn't. Frannie can't be the only one Alma had a beef with that came into the hospital that day."

"Alma was a sweet and kind person," Kappy said gently. I don't think she even had a beef, as you say, with Frannie. That was totally one-sided."

"Don't tell anyone that. It doesn't look good for Frannie."

Kappy shook her head. Edie was dramatic, no two ways about it.

Edie turned around, a plate of smooshed sandwiches in her hands. Kappy made a mental note to not let Edie handle bread and lunchmeat when she was in such a foul mood.

"Jimmy," Edie called.

Kappy could hear his footsteps on the floor above, then his rhythmic gait as he trotted down the stairs. He rushed into the kitchen and stopped short when he saw the sandwiches Edie had made.

"Is that what we're eating?" The face he made was one Kappy had seen before but was usually reserved for red foods. Here, lately, he used it for meat products.

"Ham and cheese," Edie said, tossing a bag of chips on the table. She was too preoccupied to even open them.

Kappy grabbed the bag and pulled it open.

"Ham?" Jimmy's expression turned from disgusted to horrified. "That comes from pigs; I looked it up on the Internet."

Those words seemed to bring Edie back to herself. "First of all, you can take the ham off the sandwich. I'm sorry. I forgot about the meat thing."

"It's okay." But Jimmy still didn't look like he wanted to eat the mutilated bread and cheese.

"And second of all, you can't be on the Internet unsupervised."

Jimmy sucked in a breath, his chest puffing out and his face turning red. "I'm almost twenty-one. I should be allowed on the Internet if that's what I want to do."

Edie pinched the bridge of her nose and dipped her head. "I shouldn't be having this conversation with a young Amish man."

"That's right." He gave a stern nod.

"Not because you're old enough to be on the Internet without supervision, but because *you're Amish.*"

"Still." He held his ground.

Edie shook her head, and Kappy decided

it was time to intervene.

"Why don't we talk about this later? Jimmy, you can cite the reasons why you feel you're mature enough to be on the Internet, and Edie, you can explain the dangers. Deal?"

"Yes," Edie said.

"Okay." Jimmy still seemed a little angry, but he sat down at the table and started picking at one of the sandwiches.

Edie eased into her own chair, and they started to eat. Surprisingly, the sandwiches weren't bad, just a little squashed.

"I just want to help her," Edie said. She didn't have to say who she was talking about.

"You know she'll shun you, right?"

"I know. I'm crazy, but it's eating me up that she's in jail and the real killer is out running around."

"Killer?" Jimmy asked, eyes wide.

"Sorry," Edie said.

Jimmy nodded but touched his chest where his emergency-call necklace lay.

"She shouldn't be locked up," Edie continued.

"I'm concerned for the girls. They'll have to take up her duties at the bakery as well as their own." Their business appeared to be growing. Frannie had worked hard to build it into what it was today. Then to have something like this take it all away.

"It's a shame, I tell you."

"Tomorrow's Sunday," Kappy said.

"Church Sunday," Jimmy added.

"That's right. Maybe Monday you and I can go over and help them."

"Bake?" Edie looked horrified. "I think I'd rather take my chances with Jack."

"Just for an hour or so. Then Tuesday we can go while Jimmy's at work."

"I suppose." She sounded anything but thrilled.

"It's one thing we can do to help."

"What about a food handler's permit?" Edie asked.

Kappy shot her a smile. "You don't have to have a permit to take out the trash and mop the floors."

As usual Kappy picked Jimmy up for church the following day. She drove out to the By-lers' farm and went through all the motions. All the while her thoughts were churning. There was something she was missing. Something obvious and right under her nose. Maybe so close she wasn't able to see it properly.

The Lehman daughters were in front of her on the church benches, and Kappy's

298

gaze kept straying to them. Today their shoulders held a sad, defeated slump. Murder was terrible business. And to be accused? How were they going to recover? How were they going to get their mother out of the trouble that had found them?

Or maybe the question was, how could they do something to help? Something besides take out the trash and mop the floor.

Kappy hated the feeling of powerlessness that stole over her, and she said a prayer for humbleness and perspective. She also needed to pray that God's will be done, but she couldn't form those words. What if this was God's will? But how could that be?

Somehow she managed to make it through the church service without embarrassing herself by not following the instruction for singing and prayer.

She stared down into the cup of water she held. She wished it were Kool-Aid. Edie had been making cherry Kool-Aid, and Kappy had developed a taste for it. A glass would sure taste good just now. Or maybe she just wished she was at home. Frannie's arrest was messing with her head. Kappy knew she was innocent. She didn't know how she knew, she just knew.

It all went back to the message Alma left in the flour. If they were right and nine babies meant babies born in September and ME blue was actually Emmy Blue, then perhaps she had been referring to Amelia's child that had been born in September when her own child had died.

But why would she bring that up now? Why hadn't she identified her killer in those final moments?

Realization shot through her like a bolt of lightning.

Kappy tossed her cup into the trash and went to find Jimmy. He was talking with his friend, Chris Esh, who also loved miniature pigs. Chris, the younger brother of Sally June and Jonah, had been sick most of his life and it seemed as if the time had passed him by. He was much younger than Jimmy, but they had developed a deep friendship. They each knew what it was like to be just on the outside of the circle.

"Jimmy," she called. "It's time to go." She did her best to keep the wild urgency from her voice. She didn't want to alert any of the people around them as to her anxious state. She had no idea who the daughter of Emmy Blue might be. She could have sat next to her in church this morning.

Okay maybe not this morning as she sat between the Widow Kate and Martha Peachey, who clicked her teeth during most of the preaching.

"Can't we stay a little longer?" Jimmy asked.

"Sorry, but I promised your sister we would be home by . . ." What time was it? Early but not so early that she would be suspect if she left. She checked the sun. "Two o'clock." Maybe she was close.

"Okay." He dragged his feet as he stood.

They would never get out of there if he kept moving at that pace.

"I tell you what. How about I get with Chris's mother and we come up with a time for the two of you to visit this week?"

"Can I go to his house? He has pigs."

"You have goats," Chris countered.

Two animal loving boys.

"We'll figure it out, okay?" She motioned for Jimmy to hurry. "Let's just get going for now."

She wasn't sure, but the teenager who retrieved her horse might have been the slowest human she had ever seen. He walked June Bug toward her at a snail's pace while Kappy did her best not to tap her foot impatiently. Getting annoyed and upset wouldn't get Frannie out of jail any quicker. It was Sunday. They wouldn't be able to do anything until tomorrow. That was assuming that they would find Emmy Blue's daughter.

It took all of her willpower to drive home without sending June Bug into an all-out racing stride. She had their safety to consider. Never before had she wanted to travel by car, but today . . .

In what had to be the regular time it took for her to get from the Bylers' back to her house, she had managed to calm herself a bit. Maybe it was Jimmy and his sweet, constant chatter about pigs. If he kept this up, she knew that Edie would cave and let him have them. In fact, Kappy was surprised that Edie had held out this long. His voice soothed her as he talked, and she drove. But as they neared the house her excitement and agitation renewed. She tied the reins to the hitching post Ruth had installed for business purposes and ran toward the house.

"Edie," she called as she let herself in. "Edie!"

"What?"

"I know who killed Alma."

Edie grabbed her hand, dragged her into the living room. She forced her to sit on the sofa, then took the chair opposite.

"Who?"

"Emmy Blue's daughter. That's why Alma left that message in the flour."

"She would have named her if she were

the killer."

"If she had written the daughter's name in the flour, would you know who to find?"

"Not if she didn't live here."

"Or if she got married and took her husband's name." She had heard of some English who didn't.

"We don't even have a name," Edie said miserably.

"And Emmy Blue left the Amish for the English world. Not only does she not live here, we can't access any Amish records about her birth."

Edie chuckled. "But we have the Internet. Stay right there." She jumped to her feet and raced out of the room. Kappy heard her quick footsteps on the stairs, then again and Edie was back in a flash with her laptop.

"Where do we start?" Kappy asked.

Edie placed her computer on the coffee table and made Kappy scooch over on the couch so she could sit down next to her. Edie turned on the computer and they waited. It hummed and lights came on and still they waited. It seemed like an eternity before it "booted-up," as Edie said.

"Where do we begin?" Kappy asked.

Edie sat, fingers poised over the flat of letters.

Kappy looked at the screen. A blank bar

and a little blinking line stared back at her. "Is this the Internet?" It was less wordy than she had imagined.

"It's the search engine," Edie explained. "I type something in the search bar, and it will find it for me. Or give me choices anyway."

"What are you going to type?"

"I don't know. We searched Amelia Gingerich and each one that came up was not Alma's sister. That we know."

"Well, she married, right? So she wouldn't be Amelia Gingerich anymore."

"True dat," Edie said.

"Don't start."

"Without a last name, we have nothing." Edie sat back and sighed.

They had the Internet and nothing at the same time. Kappy didn't understand how that was possible, but she didn't understand a lot, a whole big lot when computers were involved.

"What do we do?" she asked.

"I don't know." Edie stopped. "Where's Jimmy?"

"He went around to feed the animals."

"This early?"

"I sort of told him it was later than it was, so we could leave church early."

"He should have come in and changed

clothes." She shook her head. "I'll never get all those puppy paw mud stains off his white shirt."

"Sorry about that. I was so excited to get in and talk to you about this clue that I forgot all about him being in his church clothes."

As she said the words she noticed that Edie was dressed a bit differently. Maybe even a lot differently. "Are you wearing a dress?"

She stiffened. "I own dresses."

"Then how come I've never seen you in one?"

"I've just never had the occasion to wear one."

"What's the occasion today?"

Edie sniffed, her back still ramrod straight. "If you must know, I went to church."

She wouldn't have surprised Kappy more if she had said she had flown around the world in a jet and just now arrived back.

"Church?"

"Yes." Her tone took on a defensive edge. "I can go to church."

Kappy grinned. "Of course you can. There may be hope for you yet."

"I'm going to pretend you didn't say that last part."

"Fine by me." Kappy couldn't stop smiling. She was so proud of Edie. "Did Jack go with you?"

Edie turned pink, at least four shades darker than her hair. "Why would Jack go with me? We're not dating."

Maybe not, but they should be.

"You should invite him to go with you next week," Kappy said.

"Who said I was going back?"

"No one, I guess." But she had a good feeling that Edie would.

They stared at the computer screen trying to think of what to search for in order to find out anything about Emmy Blue's daughter.

"One thing's for certain, if she's here in Blue Sky, then no one knows who she is."

"Well, it's not like she's living Amish."

"Jah," Kappy said. "But we could have been standing next to her at the grocery store and never known it."

"Or she could have been our checkout girl."

"Will you be serious?"

"I am being serious. She really could have been our checkout girl." But without a name how were they supposed to find her?

"What would Sherlock Holmes do?" Kappy mused.

"Call Watson?"

"No," she said slowly. "He would solve this himself. He had a quick mind, you know."

"And he was fictional," Edie pointed out.

"Not the point," Kappy returned.

What would Holmes do? He would look at what they had as far as clues and figure out where the next could be found. How could they find the name of Amelia's child?

"Ask her uncle," Kappy said.

"What?"

"That's what Holmes would do. He would find someone who knew the woman and go ask them. He would find the next clue."

"Okay and her uncle is . . ."

"Bishop Sam," they said at the same time.

They got Jimmy out of the barn and all three climbed into Kappy's yellow buggy. For once Edie didn't protest about the slow trip. She understood as well as Kappy that they would be better welcomed in a buggy than if they had driven up in a car.

"I'll let you do the talking," Edie said. "It's not like he'll talk to me anyway."

"Probably not."

"Can I go look at his horses?" Jimmy asked.

"If he doesn't care, then it's fine with me,"

Edie said. "Just be careful."

Kappy didn't need to see it to know that Jimmy rolled his eyes at his sister. "I will."

Bishop Sam, in addition to all his other endeavors, boarded horses for other people, English and Amish alike. At any given time he had a wide variety of horses and Jimmy loved to see them every chance he got.

He was barely containing his excitement as Kappy pulled her buggy into the drive at Bishop Sam's.

He came out onto the porch as Kappy stopped the buggy. They all piled out, and Jimmy ran ahead, immediately asking if he could go look at the horses.

Bishop Sam nodded, and Jimmy took off.

"Kappy." He nodded in her direction, an invitation to announce why she had come out to his farm on this Sunday afternoon.

"Bishop Sam."

Thankfully Edie didn't pick this time to express her dislike over her *Bann.*

"I don't think Frannie Lehman is guilty," Kappy started, saying the words as gently and apologetically as she could. She had no idea how Bishop Sam felt about Frannie's arrest. It wasn't like he talked about it during the service.

"I don't, either, but I must trust that the police are doing their jobs."

She nodded. "I understand. But I also know that a person can do their job and still get it wrong from time to time."

"I agree with that." He heaved a deep breath and the buttons on his shirt stretched even farther. Kappy was surprised they didn't pop. Bishop Sam was a big man, always had been. Now that Alma was gone, would he lose weight since he wouldn't have her delicious pies to eat? Or would he somehow stay the same? Only time would tell.

Kappy shifted, wondering how to ask what needed to be asked. Best to be straight-forward. "Amelia —"

"Alma's sister?" He seemed shocked to even hear her name. Maybe Kappy was way off in her theory.

No. No room for doubts. Not when Frannie's life was hanging in the balance.

"*Jah,* the one they called Emmy Blue."

"What about her?"

"I think her daughter is who Alma was referring to in her message. The one she left in flour."

Bishop Sam blinked. He seemed so different these days. She supposed grief could do that to a person. And this was early grief, new, fresh, raw.

"Do you know her name?" Kappy gently

pressed.

"Of course. It's Barbara. Barbara Lacey. Her husband's name was Robert."

Score! That's just what she needed to know. "You wouldn't happen to know what city they live in . . . ?"

"Alma knew." His voice cracked a little at the end. "But I think they are still living in Pennsylvania somewhere. She kept in touch with her, but with me being the bishop and all . . ."

Kappy understood. He could turn a blind eye to his wife keeping company with shunned family members, but it wasn't something he himself could do in good conscience.

She smiled. "Thank you."

He gave a quick nod.

"I'll just go get Jimmy, and we'll get on our way."

"You know it's never too late to come back into the fold, Edith Peachey."

Out of the corner of her eye, Kappy saw Edie jump when he said her name. She had gotten accustomed to being ignored everywhere they went. Everywhere Amish, at least.

"Uh, thank you," Edie said, her voice soft and hesitant and very un-Edie like.

"Time spent with the English can really

make a person appreciate their Plain up-bringing," he continued. "And some think there's no coming back. But that's not true."

"I appreciate that," Edie said.

"I'll just go get Jimmy," Kappy said. "Edie?" She didn't want to leave her alone with the bishop. Things were tense enough already.

Edie nodded and started toward her.

"And Kappy King," the bishop called from behind her. "Don't think I don't know what you're up to on a Sunday afternoon."

"*Jah,* okay," she said.

But there was nothing in the *Ordnung* against solving a murder mystery on a Sunday. She was fairly certain.

She was also fairly certain that looking things up on the Internet on a Sunday would be frowned upon by the elders. Then again looking up things on the Internet on any day would be frowned upon, so there was that.

It didn't matter, though. It couldn't matter. This was a special circumstance. They had to find Emmy Blue's daughter and see if she had been in Blue Sky around the time of the murder.

"But would she have killed her own aunt?" Edie asked.

"You're always telling me that people do crazy things."

"I know, but . . ."

"But what?"

"This doesn't seem to fit. I mean, we have Alma's clue, and that part fits."

"Unless we have it wrong," Kappy said.

"I don't think so."

"Then anything can happen."

Edie nodded.

"Look her up on Facebooks."

Edie smiled. "Facebook. Singular. No *s* at the end."

"Whatever. Just look her up."

"I am."

"Can I look up someone when you're done?" Jimmy asked.

"Who do you know on Facebook?" Kappy asked.

"There's a pig farmer over in Richfield."

"Of course," Kappy said.

"He has a special deal if you like his page or something like that."

"How about we do that in a little bit?" Edie asked.

Jimmy's face lit up like an English Christmas tree. "You mean that?"

Edie turned her attention from the computer screen and settled it on her brother. "I said we would like his Facebook page.

That's all. And that doesn't mean we're getting pigs."

"Okay," Jimmy said. He sauntered away, obviously realizing that he had pushed it far enough for one day.

They might not be getting pigs tomorrow, but they were one step closer.

"Here." Edie tugged Kappy's sleeve. "This is her."

The woman staring back at them from the computer screen had a cap of soft blond curls, a round face, and blue eyes that sparkled. She was nearly the mirror image of her aunt.

"Does she look familiar?" Edie asked.

"She looks like Alma, but I don't think I've ever seen her before."

"Not at the hospital? Or maybe hanging around the Sundries and Sweets? What about at the pie-baking competition?"

Kappy shook her head. She'd had all her hopes pinned on this. Finding Emmy Blue's daughter was supposed to solve the mystery and get Frannie out of jail. Now that theory was slipping away.

"I'm not giving up so easily," Edie said. She typed in a command and waited for the computer to respond. A picture covered the screen. A smiling Barbara was holding a baby no more than four or five months old.

He was dressed entirely in blue.

"Who's that?" Kappy asked.

"Her grandbaby, I guess. Maybe a great-grandbaby."

"Is she old enough for that?"

"How would I know? It could even be the neighbor's baby."

"Right. Not what's important."

"Exactly." Edie clicked a couple of the keys on the laptop and a running stream of pictures appeared. "Maybe if we look through her photos, we'll find something."

"You can look at her pictures?"

"Yes." Edie chuckled.

"Can anyone look at them?"

"Anyone with a computer and a Facebook account."

"Huh." That seemed a little too out there for Kappy. What was private if it was all up on the computer?

"She has an open profile," Edie said.

"Okay." Kappy had no idea what that meant, but Edie acted as if that explained everything.

"Because of that, we can see all her pictures. It'll be quicker to go through them than look through her feed."

"Right." She really had no idea what Edie meant by that. Barbara Lacey had special feed? *Englishers.*

There were all kinds of pictures there. Barbara on vacation on some beach, wearing a modest bathing suit and a fruity-looking drink in each hand. There were more of her at some sort of meeting. Several of the shots had all the people lined up and turned slightly to the side. Perhaps they wanted to know who all was there that day. Pictures of a stocky little tan dog with a black face and a smooshed nose, a slinky white cat with orange striped spots, and a large golden-colored dog who looked like he was about to lick the camera.

There were pictures of children, crafts, a house, a car, pictures that looked old in black and white with creases from wear. There were holiday pictures from the Fourth of July all the way until Christmas.

And just when Kappy thought they had reached another dead end, a familiar face popped onto the screen.

Kappy looked at Edie. Edie looked at Kappy.

"We gotta call Jack," they said together.

CHAPTER 15

Less than twenty minutes later, a loud knock sounded on the front door.

"That's Jack," Kappy said and rose to let him in.

He continued to knock. Loudly. Maybe Edie's message was a little too vague. And cryptic. Maybe a bit too urgent.

He rattled the doorknob, then knocked again before Kappy could get it unlocked.

She opened the door, and Detective Jack Jones fell through over the threshold.

"What is it?" His dark gaze raced over her, looking for injury or blood. Maybe both.

"Come in and sit down," Kappy said.

Those words drew him back. "Where's Edie?"

Kappy pointed toward the living room. "In there."

"And she's okay?"

"Jah."

"But her message —"

"We're talking about Edie here."

"Right." Jack braced his hands on his hips and sucked in a deep breath. When he let it go, he seemed to deflate a little, as if the tension of thinking one of them might be hurt had puffed him up beyond his normal size.

"Jack!" Edie called. "Come in here."

Kappy smiled. "You're being summoned."

"And no one's hurt?"

Kappy shook her head.

"Or maimed?"

"No."

"Bleeding? Murdered?"

"No and no," Kappy said.

"Then this better be good." He cut to the left and entered the living room where Edie waited.

Kappy followed behind.

"What is going on?" he asked, flopping down in the large chair next to the couch.

"We know who murdered Alma Miller."

"Yes, we all do."

"You're talking about Frannie Lehman, but she isn't guilty."

"It's looking bad for her from where I'm standing. But guilt or innocence is up for the jury to decide. I just bring them in."

"But you brought in the wrong one this time."

He looked to Kappy as if she might help, might be the voice of reason. She couldn't play that part today. "Show him," she said.

Edie turned the computer around so Jack could see what they had found.

"Who's that?"

"Amelia Gingerich Porter."

"The infamous Emmy Blue. Didn't we discover she was dead?" Jack asked.

"That's right, but this woman isn't." She reached around the side of the computer and clicked a couple more buttons. A younger face, much like the first one appeared on the screen.

The similarities were such that Kappy couldn't believe she hadn't seen them until now. That cheery smile and so-bright blue eyes. Well, Kappy had seen them. They had been bugging her for days, but she couldn't cite a reason for those nagging feelings until today.

"Who is that?" he asked.

"You don't recognize her?" Edie raised her brows in a silent challenge.

"Should I?"

The picture of Bobbie Jean wasn't the best nor was it of good lighting. And she was heavier, much heavier, confirming Kappy's theory that she had a chore in keeping her weight down.

"That's Bobbie Jean Hawkins."

"The judge from Mrs. O'Malley's Pies." He nodded.

"And daughter of Emmy Blue's September baby." Kappy said the words and waited for him to express his gratitude. They had done it again.

"Barbara Jean, not Roberta. She was named for her mother, Barbara Porter Lacey," Edie added. "But nicknamed Bobbie."

"Let me get this straight . . . are you saying you believe that she killed Alma Miller?"

"Yes," Edie said.

"Based on?"

"Alma's message in the flour, for one."

"I think your reasoning is sound, but that doesn't mean it's correct. The one thing we 'know' about Alma's message is that we don't really know what it says. It's all speculation, and speculation can't hold in court. There has to be proof." He shifted in his seat as if no longer comfortable. "Listen, I really appreciate you two trying to help."

Funny, he said the words, but it just didn't sound like he really meant them.

"I hear a *but.*" Edie waited for him to continue.

"I am not at liberty to tell you everything

I know about this case. But I can tell you that I have a witness who saw Frannie Lehman leave the hospital in a hurry around the same time Alma passed away."

"What witness?" Edie asked. "Who is it?"

Jack shot her a look, that *you know better than to think I can answer that* sort of look that he seemed to give her a lot.

"Edie, we have our man, so to speak. But I do appreciate you calling me." He rose to his feet as if he was about to leave.

"You're not leaving," Edie said. It was more of a statement than a question.

"I am." He stretched out his long legs and started from the room.

"Seriously?" Edie called after him.

"Thanks for the effort," Jack called from the foyer. The front door opened, then closed, and he was gone.

"That man!" Edie growled.

That man indeed.

"I don't understand," Kappy said the next day. She had spent an almost sleepless night mulling over what Jack had told them about the murder scene and —

"We need proof," Edie said.

"What kind of proof?"

"I don't know. Proof-proof."

Kappy shook her head. Leave it to Edie to

so eloquently express herself. "I thought what we had was pretty good."

"Evidently it's not good enough for you-know-who."

"So what do we do?"

Edie shook her head. "I was hoping you would have an idea."

"Let me think."

"What would Sherlock Holmes do?" Edie asked.

"He would be quiet so I could think."

"Right." Edie shut her mouth, then lips pressed tightly together, she pretended to turn a key and toss it over one shoulder.

"Bobbie Jean Hawkins is probably long gone," Kappy mused.

Edie nodded mutely.

"If she *is* staying in town, no one knew where she was before the competition, so it's likely that no one knows where she is now."

Edie nodded again.

"What we need is motive," Kappy said.

Edie nodded.

"Would you stop that?"

"Sorry. I thought you wanted quiet."

"I do," Kappy said, "but I also need few distractions. You nodding your head like one of those bobbly dogs people put on the dash of their cars is definitely a distraction."

"Sorry," Edie mumbled again.

"Where was I?" Kappy asked.

"Motive."

"Right. That's one thing that Jack has on Frannie that we don't have for Bobbie Jean."

"But if she did it, there would have to be a motive."

"The pie recipe," Kappy said slowly.

"I thought you said pie couldn't be a motive for murder."

"I might have been wrong." The wheels in her mind started turning, and she was having a tough time keeping up with her own thoughts. "Bobbie Jean works for a pie company."

"Yes."

"What if the rumors are true and she was here to look for a pie recipe? Not a new one, but an old one."

Edie blinked, the theory starting to come into focus. "Her great-aunt's recipe."

"Jah."

"But didn't Rose tell us that Emmy Blue had the recipe?"

"If she died without writing it down or passing it on, then Alma was her only choice."

"Then why kill her?"

"I think it was a crime of passion. Bobbie

Jean's job is on the line. This is her birth-right."

"So when Alma wouldn't give her the recipe, she decided to take it."

"She hit Alma on the head with the frying pan or whatever, then ran out with the recipe box."

"But the recipe wasn't in there."

"Right," Kappy said. "And when Alma started to come out of her coma, she refused to give her the recipe again."

"And Bobbie Jean killed her." Edie shook her head at it all. "What about the quilt from the bed?"

"Another heirloom, so to speak."

"But if she killed Alma and Alma had never written down the recipe, then . . ." She cut off and they looked at each other.

"The bakery," they said at the same time.

Kappy glanced to the back seat where Jimmy sat. She felt bad about bringing him along, but how dangerous could this be? They were going to warn the Lehman girls and all the bakery workers to keep an eye out for Bobbie Jean. Frannie's recipe was as close as anything could be to the original. Kappy was reluctant to say identical, but they were very similar. Very, *very* similar.

Then once they talked to Susie, Rosie M,

and Amanda, they were heading straight over to talk to Jack Jones again. There was too much at stake here for them to leave it alone.

Edie pulled her car to the side of the road in front of the house, and the three got out. Thankfully, no other cars were parked nearby, and Kappy could hope that no one else was inside. They needed to talk, but without witnesses.

Together Jimmy, Edie, and Kappy walked around the side of the house and down the basement stairs. They let themselves in, hesitating for a moment just inside the door, waiting for their eyes to adjust to the new lighting. As she had hoped, the bakery was currently empty. But for how long was anybody's guess.

"Hi, Kappy King, what brings you out today?"

"Hi, Susie." Kappy made her way over to the counter and the eldest Lehman daughter. Edie trailed behind while Jimmy started examining the decorated sugar cookies. "Do you still have your *mamm*'s recipe book?"

She shook her head. "That dark cop took it."

"Jack Jones?"

"Maybe. Why?"

"I was hoping to take a quick look at it,

but if you don't have it any longer . . ." Then the recipe was completely safe, locked in the evidence room at the sheriff's office. If there were such a thing. An evidence room, not a sheriff's office. She knew the sheriff's office was real.

"Listen." Edie took a couple of steps forward, her posture intense, her manner so electric that the girls couldn't help but listen to her. "We know your *mamm* is innocent, but we can't prove it yet."

"If she's innocent, why is she still in jail?"

No one seemed to care that Edie was under the *Bann*. The girls behind the counter talked to them — both of them — like they had done this very same thing every day.

"Good question," Kappy said. "There's some evidence against her —"

"Purely circumstantial," Edie interrupted.

"Yes," Kappy agreed.

"But enough to hold her in the jail," Rosie M said.

"I'm afraid so," Kappy said. "But there's something else. We think Bobbie Jean Hawkins actually killed Alma."

"The pie lady killed the bishop's wife?" Susie shook her head.

"Why would she do that?" Amanda asked.

"Bobbie Jean is Alma's great-niece," Edie

325

explained. "She's the daughter of Emmy Blue's daughter."

The sisters frowned as if assimilating the information and working through all the relations. It was quite a puzzle.

"She felt she deserved the recipe, and Alma wouldn't let her have it. She didn't want it exploited by mass production." Kappy didn't know for certain, but she had a strong feeling that had been the reason. Bobbie Jean hadn't wanted that family recipe for the holidays; she wanted it to keep her job.

"We think she might come by here and try to steal your mom's new recipe."

"Why would she do that?" Amanda asked.

"Because *Mamm*'s new recipe tastes just like Alma's," Susie supplied.

"And it would be a hit at Mrs. O'Malley's," Rosie M added.

The girls were catching on.

"And it's available." Not locked in the minds of two deceased women.

"Especially since good ol' Frannie is locked away in jail."

The five women plus Jimmy turned as a new voice entered the conversation. They had been so busy talking that they hadn't heard anyone else come in.

Bobbie Jean Hawkins stood at the door of

the bakery, a sinister grin spread across her round face. Her blue eyes so like those of her great-aunt weren't sparkling now but narrowed in deceit.

"Why are you here?" Edie asked.

Bobbie Jean laughed. "I want the recipe. I've worked hard enough for it."

Edie scoffed. Kappy shot her a look.

Something was off in Bobbie Jean's actions. Maybe it was desperation, maybe it was greed. Kappy hoped it was the latter. A stingy person was easier to deal with than one who was desperate.

"You haven't worked any for it," Edie said, ignoring Kappy's silent warning.

"I shouldn't have to work for it at all. That recipe is my birthright after all."

"Your birthright?" Rosie M asked, a frown in her brow.

Bobbie Jean's attention shifted from Edie to Rosie M. There was definitely something sinister in that look. Both Amanda and Susie stepped forward to shield Rosie M and the tiny unborn Lehman she carried.

"We don't have the recipe," Susie said. "The police do."

"I don't believe for a minute that they have the only copy. You have to have some sort of recipe card or something around here. This was your mother's business. I know how it goes."

Amanda and Susie exchanged a look.

"See here." Bobbie Jean waved one hand toward the sisters. It was then that Kappy realized she had one hand in her purse and had since she had come into the bakery. "Sharing secrets means there's another copy of the recipe here. Where?"

Kappy couldn't take her eyes of Bobbie Jean's bag. It was a canvas tote with soft sides. But Kappy couldn't tell if she had a gun in it or not. Why else would she have one hand hidden that way? But the small amount of light filtering through the windows at the top of the bakery walls wasn't enough for her to see many details. True shapes were hidden in shadows. Maybe if she could get a little closer. She inched a bit forward and to her left. Bobbie Jean swung around.

Kappy could now see the mad look in her eyes. Desperation. Hen's teeth! They were not catching a break today. *Lord be with us,* she prayed. They were definitely going to need Him.

"Stay right where you are, nosy Kappy King."

Kappy's eyes widened in surprise. How did Bobbie Jean Hawkins know who she was? Or maybe the question was why? Why did Bobbie Jean Hawkins know who she was?

"I started watching you the moment I got into town. Always a little left of center but somehow in the middle of everything. I've heard the stories. But this is one crime you're not going to solve. However, if you play your cards right, you'll be able to tell the police after I'm long gone."

"No one's giving you the recipe," Edie said. "So you might as well get out of here now."

"Oh, I'm getting the recipe." She patted her tote bag. "I get the recipe, or someone gets hurt." She flashed an evil grin toward Kappy. "That's right. I have a gun in my bag. And I will use it. It'll be much easier to kill someone with a gun. So much less personal than standing next to their hospital bed with them too helpless to stop you from putting something nasty into their IV."

"I don't believe you have a gun," Edie said.

What was she doing?

"Show it to us," Edie commanded.

"I don't care if you believe I have a gun or not. Just as long as they do." She whirled around, pointing what could be considered the business end of her gun/bag toward the counter and the Lehman girls.

They all ducked, as if the gun could accidentally go off any second.

"And they believe." Bobbie Jean smiled. "Up."

Kappy could see the women through the display case as Amanda and Susie stood. Rosie M, with all that extra weight in her middle, had lost her balance and was sprawled on the floor.

The sisters grabbed one of her arms and hoisted her to her feet.

"Now, then," Bobbie Jean said. "Let's start that again."

"Ooohh," a low groan sounded from behind them. Jimmy was nearly doubled in half, clutching his midsection. "The cookies I ate," he moaned.

Edie stared at her brother. "You ate a cookie?" she asked.

Still bent at the waist one hand clutching at his belly, Jimmy held up the other with all four fingers showing.

"Four? You ate four cookies?"

Head down, he nodded.

When had he had time to eat four cookies? And how had he gotten them?

Kappy's gaze trailed toward the showcase where the cookies were displayed. The trays were all full, no empty spots. If he ate cookies, they weren't from Frannie's Bakery.

Edie started toward him.

Bobbie Jean swung the bag in her direction.

She stopped, gestured toward Jimmy. "I just want to see about my brother."

Bobbie Jean's gazed raked over them both, then she nodded.

Kappy was sure she was assessing the dangers in letting them be side by side.

"Come on," Edie said, wrapping one arm around his back.

"Ooohhh," he groaned again.

She turned him toward the one chair in the room. It sat in the far corner and would get him out of harm's way. Susie and Amanda still stood in front of Rosie M. This was what Edie could do for her brother.

"My belly hurts." Jimmy sounded so much like a small child that Kappy almost didn't believe it was him.

"You'll feel better once you sit down. Kappy, help me."

Kappy was all too aware of Bobbie Jean and the possible gun she had in her bag and the fact that it was pointed at the three of them.

Together, with Jimmy's feet nearly dragging across the concrete floor, Kappy and Edie managed to get him to the chair and turned around. They supported his elbows as his eyes closed and he dropped into the seat. He moaned loudly.

What a time for him to have a stomachache!

"Please don't kill us," Jimmy begged. "I don't want to die in a basement bakery." His eyes opened and settled on Kappy. Then he winked before closing them and moaning once more.

"He's down, now get back over here."

Wait. Had he really just winked?

She looked to Edie, but she showed no signs of having seen anything at all. Maybe Kappy had simply imagined it.

Kappy and Edie moved away from Jimmy and back where Bobbie Jean pointed. Kappy wanted to look back more than Lot's wife and see if Jimmy was faking. Or really in pain. If he was faking, then why?

He groaned, and Bobbie Jean rolled her eyes. "Just what I needed today." She turned her full attention back to the Lehmans. "Have you decided who's going to get me that recipe? I've waited long enough."

Kappy mentally calculated the time that they had been in the bakery. It seemed like hours. But it could have only been minutes. But how many? Frannie's Bakery was a busy place. How long before some unsuspecting customer came down those stairs expecting to get a cupcake and instead getting a bullet? They needed to get Bobbie Jean out of there and fast.

She looked to Susie. Kappy caught her gaze tried to tell her with her eyes to hand over the recipe. It wasn't worth dying for, no matter that Alma already had.

But Susie just stared blankly at her.

From behind her, Kappy heard Jimmy shift in his seat. He was completely out of Bobbie's Jean's line of vision. Was he going to rush her? Maybe that was why he faked a stomachache caused by four cookies he never ate. He had the advantage now being behind Kappy and Edie, almost hidden from Bobbie Jean. But was he fast enough? She didn't think so. *Lord, please keep him there.* For the first time in her life she wished someone a stomachache, a real one that would prevent him from doing something really stupid.

How long before someone came down those stairs?

"Listen, I can do this all day," Bobbie Jean boasted. "I hung a closed sign on the door and locked it on my way in. No one's coming down here. Poor Frannie has been arrested; of course the bakery is closed."

Kappy wasn't sure if she was relieved or disappointed. That could have been the one thing to save them. In the right scenario, say Jack figured out they were telling him the truth about Frannie and decided to come talk to the girls himself. Then he would have been the one coming down the stairs. And since she knew he had a gun, the odds would be more even for certain.

What would Sherlock Holmes do?

He wouldn't have found himself locked in a basement bakery by a mad woman with a gun.

No.

He would assess the situation. Find the weakness of the criminal. Everyone had a weakness. Then he would exploit it to his benefit.

What was Bobbie Jean's weakness?

"Come now," she urged. "I truly have all day. But I don't want to spend all day. We get this done quick enough and I might have time for a mani-pedi. After I skip town, of course."

That was it! She thought she was going to just walk away from all this. Go back to her life and continue on like nothing happened. Like she didn't leave five . . . *six* witnesses behind.

Kappy wondered if Bobbie Jean had thought that far ahead. Probably not, but with the murderous look in her eyes and that off-kilter smile she wore, Kappy wasn't about to bring it up. But the other . . .

"You get the recipe, what then?"

"I get my job back at O'Malley's."

"You lost your job?" Edie asked. "That's what all this is about?"

"I worked so hard to scrape my way up in the company. I started there right out of high school. Went to college at night to get my MBA and move up. I made VP and all this craziness happened. They fired me. But if I have this recipe, they will beg me to come back."

"You really think so?" Kappy asked.

"Why would you want to work for someone who fired you?" Edie asked.

"So I had an affair with the boss. He got demoted and I got fired. How's that fair?"

"It's not. But neither is stealing a recipe that doesn't belong to you," Edie said.

"How was any of this fair to Alma?" Jimmy asked. His voice was surprisingly clear for someone with such a belly-ache. Maybe Kappy hadn't imagined that wink after all.

"Alma deserved it." Bobbie Jean lifted her chin as if daring one of them to contradict her.

"Why?" Edie asked.

Behind the counter the Lehmans shifted,

moving a little toward the side of the bakery farthest from the door.

"That recipe was my birthright. My grandmother had just as much ownership of it."

"So why didn't she give it to you?" Edie asked.

"She died when I was a baby."

"And she didn't give it to your mother?" Kappy asked.

"My mother was never interested in baking."

"You took the quilt." Kappy's voice was filled with the wonder of understanding.

"It was my quilt. Well, it would have been. My great-grandmother took it from Amelia when she left to go live English. If she hadn't done that, the quilt would have been passed down to me."

"And that's worth a woman's life?"

"Two women," Susie spoke up. The girls had moved all the way to the far corner. They had Rosie M behind them as they stood like guardians of the future.

"Two?" Bobbie Jean shook her head. "How do you figure that?"

"If you let our mother take the blame for your crime."

Bobbie Jean scoffed. "I can't worry about that." She pointed to Susie. "You seem like the leader. Where's that recipe?"

That's when it happened. Just for a moment Susie's gaze strayed to some point behind them. Jimmy. Kappy half turned to check on him.

He nodded his head, pointed from Kappy to Bobbie Jean, then toward the door of the shop. Then he rubbed his chin.

What in the world was he doing? Trying to give her a message, but what?

He repeated the motion, then added one more. He pointed to his sister and then to Bobbie Jean.

He wanted them to jump her. If they did it at the same time, they could take her down.

"She . . . she keeps them in her office," Susie said.

"Nice try, but I'm not letting you out of here without that recipe in my hand." Bobbie Jean scoffed. "In her office. What good are recipes if you're in an office?"

"Aren't you taking it to an office?" Susie asked.

"Not the same," Bobbie Jean singsonged.

With her attention on Susie, Kappy stared at Edie until she shifted her attention to return the look.

Kappy made a series of pointing gestures, hoping that Edie could understand them.

If she was reading Jimmy's made-up sign

language, then they were to jump Bobbie Jean because Jack was coming. But that last part had Kappy stumped. How did Jack even know they were there?

"Listen, are you going to cooperate or am I going to have to start shooting people? I could start with your sister." Bobbie Jean cocked her head toward where Rosie M was leaning in the corner.

"No. It's all right. I'll get the recipes." Susie made her way to the opposite end of the display counter, the end closest to the door of the shop. She opened the cabinet there and started rifling through the contents. Kappy wasn't sure if she was really going to hand over the recipe or if she was merely stalling for time.

With Bobbie Jean's attention centered on Susie, it was the perfect time to make their move.

Kappy caught Edie's gaze. She nodded in return, and Kappy silently counted it off on her fingers. When she reached one, they both lunged at Bobbie Jean. The woman screamed as they tackled her from behind. A shot rang out. Susie screamed and hit the floor behind the counter. In the corner, Rosie M slid down the wall, eyes closed. Was she hit? Amanda screamed and ducked out of sight.

Then stuff really started happening. The door to the bakery burst open and Jack Jones ran inside.

CHAPTER 16

"You?" Edie stared at her brother with wide, incredulous eyes. "You did this?" She gestured toward the chaos that surrounded them in Frannie's Bakery.

Bobbie Jean had been taken into custody, handcuffed, and transported to the jail. She had only brought a kid's cap gun as a weapon. Most probably bought that very morning at the dry goods store.

An ambulance had been called for Rosie M, but word had come back quickly that she was fine. She had merely locked her knees during the exchange and had passed out. Amanda and Susie had been taken to the station with the honey-haired detective that worked with Jack. Kappy had learned that her name was Sam, short for Samantha, Johnson. Kappy filed her name away as Detective Sam on the off-chance that they might meet again.

Jimmy apparently was perfectly okay.

Which didn't surprise Kappy. She had suspected all along that he hadn't eaten four cookies and couldn't have a bellyache.

He continued to grin. "I bent over and pretended to be sick, but I was really pressing the button on my emergency necklace." His expression fell. "That's okay, right? This was enough of an emergency, *jah*?"

Jack Jones laughed. "Definitely."

"I turned the microphone on but turned off the speaker. They could hear us, but we couldn't hear them."

Now his begging for his life in a "bakery basement" made sense. He had been tipping off the dispatcher as to where they were. There was only one basement bakery in Blue Sky and it belonged to Frannie Lehman.

"That was really smart of you," Edie said. Kappy could tell that she wanted to hug him, but she was doing her best to control her emotions and keep her hands at her sides.

"And really brave." The praise from Jack made Jimmy's smile all the brighter.

"Now what?" Kappy asked.

"Everybody will need to come to the station and make a statement, but from here it's pretty cut and dry. Bobbie Jean will stand trial for Alma's murder and probably

341

go to prison for the rest of her life."

And maybe then, things would settle down in Blue Sky.

Two days later Kappy was outside with Elmer harvesting the last of her fall vegetables. They were due for a hard freeze any day now and anything left on the vines would most likely perish in the cold. Fall had taken hold, but winter was coming.

Elmer sat down on his rear and tossed his nose into the air. Ears back and eyes closed, he started his howling bark. Someone was out front.

Kappy set her hoe to the side and wiped her hands on her apron, smearing it with dirt but not managing to get much off her hands.

She let herself out of the backyard, using one foot to keep Elmer inside while she went to investigate.

A bright yellow buggy sat in her drive. Frannie Lehman was climbing down.

"If you want a covering, go around back, down the basement."

Frannie touched her prayer *kapp* as if she needed reminding it was there.

Kappy started to turn away and get back to her work. She and Frannie had never been anything more than two people who

342

lived in the same church district. She didn't see that changing now.

"I didn't come for a covering. Can you ride with me up to the Peacheys'?"

"Martha's?"

She gently shook her head, a small smile playing at the corners of her lips. It was so tiny and so unexpected that Kappy was confused as to if she had even seen it at all. "Edie and Jimmy's."

Kappy tried not to look completely shocked. "Uh, okay." She looked down at her hands, then tried to brush some of the dirt from her apron. "Let me just —"

"Come as you are," Frannie said. "I'm sure Edie will allow you to clean up once we're there."

Kappy looked around, as if she was searching for an excuse not to go. But why? Elmer was safely in the backyard so her neighbor's plants and chickens should be in no danger. For the time being anyhow. There was nothing on in the house. The water wasn't running by her garden. There was no reason to back up and say no.

"*Jah.*" She couldn't help herself. She brushed at her hands and wiped at her apron, but it was all in vain.

Frannie smiled a bit, nodded her head, and climbed into the buggy.

They rode in silence on the short trip to Edie and Jimmy's. Silence was a relative term considering the amount of noise the dogs made when a strange buggy pulled up. A person would think they would get used to strange vehicles, but that was just the way beagles were. Beautiful, noisy creatures.

Frannie tied her horse to the hitching post and together they made their way up the porch steps. Kappy gave a quick knock, then opened the door.

"Kappy!" A delighted Jimmy met them as they stepped into the foyer. But he drew up short when he realized that she wasn't alone. The smile took over once again as he recognized who she had with her.

"Frannie. I love your cookies. Do you know how to bake a lemon cake with all this fancy swirly icing?"

Frannie shrugged. "I suppose so. But today I brought pie."

Her words seemed to insinuate that there would be other times with different desserts.

"Cool." He turned and headed for the kitchen. "Edie, Frannie is here and she brought pie." He said the words as if this were the most natural occurrence in the world.

"She is?" Edie came out of the downstairs bathroom, pulling Coke-can-sized rollers from her hair. Kappy would have wondered what such big contraptions would do for shorter hair, but the look was actually cute.

"Are you going somewhere?" Kappy asked.

"Jack's on his way." Jimmy's tone carried a tune.

"Oh, *jah*?"

"It's not what you think," Edie said. "He called and said he had something for Jimmy."

Kappy nodded. "Oh." So of course Edie was making the best of the situation. Fixing her hair, wearing makeup, and dressing a little more like the old Edie. Cherry-red pants, a pale pink top with a large red heart right in the middle, and a pair of flat shoes covered with beads and jewels.

"I'm sorry," Frannie said. "I should have told you that I wanted to come over first."

"It's fine. Come on in." She took the last roller from her hair and ran her fingers through the pastel curls.

"She has pie," Jimmy said, his enthusiasm palpable.

"I wanted to say thank you for helping me get out of jail and saving my bakery." Her eyes started to tear. "Protecting my girls."

"Don't cry." Kappy and Edie watched in utter shock as Jimmy wrapped one arm about Frannie's shoulders and directed her toward the dining table. "It's all over now."

They followed them into the room.

"Everyone is safe," Jimmy reminded her. "Everyone is safe."

Frannie sniffed and wiped her eyes on her apron. "I know." She smiled up at Jimmy. "And all because of you."

Jimmy smiled but shook his head. "Nah. Not me." His face filled with color, close to the shade of his sister's shirt. "I'm not a hero."

Frannie grabbed his arm. "But you are. Rosie M and Danny are talking about naming the baby after you."

"Really?" Jimmy looked so proud that he was about to explode.

A knock sounded at the door.

Edie yelped. "That's Jack. Kappy, can you get that?"

"Of course," Kappy said, but she shook her head as her friend ducked back into the bathroom for one last look before Jack came in.

"Hi, Kappy." Jack stepped over the threshold and jerked a thumb over his shoulder. "That's not your buggy."

Frannie appeared at the doorway to the dining room. "It's mine."

"Frannie Lehman. How are you?" Jack

smiled as he said the words, but the tension was still there.

"I'm fine thank you. And thanks to you."

Evidently there were no hard feelings about Frannie's arrest, but that was to be expected.

"Glad to hear it." Jack visibly relaxed. "Are you having a party? I can come back."

Edie appeared from the bathroom, her lips shinier than when she had gone in. "No, that's fine. Come on in. I'll put on some coffee."

Fifteen minutes later everyone was seated around the table. Frannie had cut the pie she had brought and had served everyone a slice.

"Boysenberry," Edie said. "Is this the prize winner?"

Frannie gave them a mysterious smile. "You tell me."

Kappy and Jimmy were the only two at the table who had recently been fortunate to have a piece of Alma's famous boysenberry pie.

Jack and Edie looked at them expectantly.

"That's not the same," Kappy said.

"But it's good," Jimmy added. "Really good."

"Danki."

"What's different about it?" Edie asked as

she took her first bite.

"Tastes good to me," Jack said around his own mouthful.

"I can't tell you that," Frannie said. "If it gets around, everyone will be using my secret next year."

"Is this the pie you entered in the competition?" Jack asked.

She shook her head. "No, and I'm ashamed of that." She eased down into her chair and took a careful sip of her coffee. "I've spent years trying to make my pie like Alma's and trying to beat her. Now that she's gone, I realized it would have been more beneficial if I hadn't worried so much about pie and had just been her friend."

"Amen," Kappy said.

"But you discovered her recipe," Edie asked.

"Yes. But this is the pie I'll be entering next year."

"And what about Alma's recipe?" Jack asked.

"That's Alma's and should stay with her."

"Are you saying what I think you're saying?" Kappy asked.

"I took the recipe to the cemetery and buried it next to where her marker will go. It's the only copy I have."

Kappy smiled. It was almost a good ending to the story. It would have been better if Frannie had realized these things long ago.

Jimmy raised his fork. "To new recipes," he said.

Everyone lifted their fork toward the center in toast. "To new recipes," they all said.

"On the phone you said you had something for Jimmy," Edie reminded Jack.

"Oh, yeah. I almost forgot." He reached behind him in his chair and brought out a small frame. With everything going on when he arrived, no one had noticed that he carried it.

"Sam made this for you."

Jimmy smiled. "I like Detective Sam."

Jack held it up where they could see it. " 'To James Amos Peachey, for bravery and quick thinking in the line of duty,' " he read.

"What is it?" Edie asked.

"It's a Certificate of Merit."

"For me?" Jimmy couldn't contain his smile.

"For you," Jack said. Next to it he laid a small plastic badge. HONORARY SHERIFF. "I truly believe the streets of Blue Sky are a little safer today and all because of you."

Kappy smiled. They were indeed safer. For now . . .

ABOUT THE AUTHOR

Amy Lillard is an award-winning author of over forty novels and novellas ranging from Amish romance and mysteries to contemporary and historical romance. Since receiving a Carol Award for her debut novel, *Saving Gideon* (2012), she has become known for writing sweet stories filled with family values, honest characters, a hometown feel and close-knit communities. She is a member of RWA, ACFW, NINC, and the Author's Guild. Born and bred in Mississippi, she now lives with her husband and son in Oklahoma. Please visit her online at www.AmyWritesRomance.com.

The employees of Thorndike Press hope you have enjoyed this Large Print book. All our Thorndike, Wheeler, and Kennebec Large Print titles are designed for easy reading, and all our books are made to last. Other Thorndike Press Large Print books are available at your library, through selected bookstores, or directly from us.

For information about titles, please call:
(800) 223-1244

or visit our website at:
gale.com/thorndike

To share your comments, please write:
Publisher
Thorndike Press
10 Water St., Suite 310
Waterville, ME 04901